THE SHADOW OF ROBBERS' ROOST

By the same author

Chief Takes Over

Cowboy Joe of the Circle S

Ghost Cat

The Lost Treasure Box

Ponca, Cowpony

(all published by Harcourt, Brace)

YOUNG AMERICA BOOK CLUB

A Division of Weekly Reader Children's Book Club

PRESENTS

The Shadow of
Robbers' Roost

by HELEN RUSHMORE

ILLUSTRATED BY *Albert Orbaan*

CLEVELAND AND NEW YORK

THE WORLD PUBLISHING COMPANY

PUBLISHED BY The World Publishing Company
2231 West 110th Street, Cleveland 2, Ohio

PUBLISHED SIMULTANEOUSLY IN CANADA BY
Nelson, Foster & Scott Ltd.

Library of Congress Catalog Card Number: 60-7200

Young America Book Club Edition

To Happy—

and those days in the Black Mesa country

ACKNOWLEDGMENT

I am indebted to Alice Emery, who shared so generously with me many family legends concerning the boy, Buddy Emery (Jonny in this story), and the outlaw William Coe. Also I wish to thank Robert J. French. Without his guidance I would never have known the grand beauty of the Black Mesa country. Through the tales of these friendly people the outlaws of Robbers' Roost rose again, and the Canyon Road echoed the thudding hoofbeats of their phantom horses.

Contents

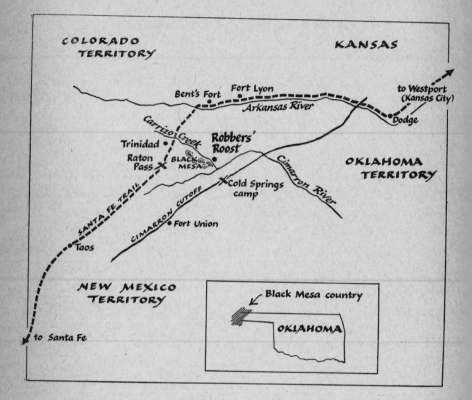

The Black Mesa Country

1

Out of the Night

"JONNY, don't wait any longer. I've spoken to you twice." Mrs. Hardy turned from the stove where she was stirring the potatoes. "Go do the chores and I'll hold supper. It's way past milking time and Charlie's been bawling this last hour."

Jonny lit the lantern and picked up the milk pail. The night was blacker than the inside of a pocket. The moon hadn't risen and in the early darkness he couldn't see the barn or the corral fence or even the clump of piñon trees by the well curb.

At the door he hesitated, looking into the soft blackness. Then he turned to his sister, Jennie, who was setting the table.

"Want to help me?" he asked hopefully.

"She's got other things to do," answered his mother. "Charlie is your yearling and milking's your chore. Now, go."

Matt looked up from the house he was building with chips from the woodbox. He grinned slyly through his curls. "Jonny's scared of the dark," he said. "That's why he wants Jennie to go with him. Jonny is a fraidy-cat. Jonny is a fraidy-cat."

Jonny flushed. Matt had a way of singing that silly chant that always set his blood boiling.

"Shut up, you little pest," he shouted, swinging the milk pail in Matt's direction. "I'll trim you down to size."

"Ma, Jonny's going to hit me," yelled Matt. "Make him stop."

"Shame on you, Jonny." Mrs. Hardy's voice was tired, but her eyes snapped impatiently. "A big boy like you talking like that to your little brother. Sometimes I'm hard put to remember you're twelve years old."

Jonny slammed the door but not soon enough to shut out Matt's taunting laugh. He could have reminded Ma he'd be thirteen in another month, but it would only have brought down another torrent of words.

He stomped down the path and stumbled over a rock he knew was there. It hurt his toe like sixty but not half as bad as Ma hurt when she took up for that pesky little troublemaker.

What had got into Ma? Was she blind and deaf that she didn't know Matt was the orneriest five-year-old in the Cimarron Canyon country? She ought to see the way he carried on at Pa's trading post. The way he strutted around like a gamecock, out-fighting and out-bragging any two young ones his

size, was enough to shame a cow. Besides, Jonny
was getting dad-rotted tired of fighting the big
brothers of all the little boys that Matt tied into.

Yet there were other times when the little tyke
was so mannerly Jonny was downright proud of him.
All the ladies who came into the post patted him
on the head and wished their little boys were like
him.

But let both Pa and Jonny get busy and the little
show-off started. Like the last time William Coe,
the outlaw, rode into town. Coe had always liked
Matt, and he never came without bringing him a
present. Of course Matt thought Captain Coe hung
the moon and poked holes in the sky for the stars
to shine through. He had swaggered around the post
beside Coe, copying his arrogant walk, the quick
way he turned his head, and his insulting manner
of speaking. The drovers lounging in the post hadn't
helped matters either. They'd laughed and told Matt
smart-aleck remarks to repeat when, heaven knows,
he could think up enough of his own.

He was bad enough at home when Coe and other
travelers stopped for a bite of Ma's good home
cooking and a bed in the bunkhouse. But she'd
hide her face in shame if she could see him at the
post when Jonny couldn't ride herd on him. Then
she wouldn't always be blaming him for the little
rooster's antics.

Jonny threw the lantern light on the barn-door
latch. His anger disappeared as he thought of the

big longhorn steer waiting for him inside. There was no room within him for anything but keen delight when he was with Charlie. When he worked late at Pa's post or in the fields, Jennie brought the steer in from the pasture and locked the door.

In spite of Matt's taunt, it wasn't the dark Jonny dreaded. Always in the back of his mind there was the fear that some night he might find Charlie missing. He never opened the door that he didn't remember the man up near Rabbit Ears Mountain who went into the barn and found an eight-foot puma crouched over his dead cow.

Too, now that spring was here the Indians would be moving into the canyon, setting up summer camps along the Cimarron. They still felt that the land and everything on it belonged to them. A longhorn like Charlie would look mighty good to them.

But Jonny's greatest fear was of rustlers. So far the outlaws of Robbers' Roost hadn't raided the Hardy ranch or the neighboring farms and ranches. For some reason known only to themselves, Captain Coe and his raiders had maintained a truce of sorts in this part of the Cimarron Canyon.

But often Jonny's spine chilled listening to the tales told by the cattle drovers and freighters who traveled the Santa Fe Trail, particularly those who drove the Cimarron Cutoff. This branch of the trail led through No-Man's-Land, almost within the shadow of the Black Mesa where the hideout known as Robbers' Roost was hidden.

Jonny couldn't picture the friendly well-dressed

man—who played so gently with Matt—as captain
of that band of thieves and murderers who terror-
ized the territories. Captain Coe was always kind
to Ma and Jennie and paid well for his meals.

Still the tales had to be true. There was too much
talk, too many witnesses, too many families without
fathers and brothers, to leave doubts and questions.

Jed Wilson, the old mountain man who hung around
the post, said vigilante committees were being or-
ganized up Colorado way. So far there had been
no such talk around here, or Jonny would have
heard. All the ranchers came to Pa with their troubles,
and all the rumors, both true and false, reached the
post. Everyone knew how dead set Pa was against
vigilantes taking the law into their own hands.

Coe and his men came and went freely. It was
true they were overbearing and ordered the men in
the village about as if they owned them, body and
soul. Still, they kept their guns in the holsters, and
so far no one had lost any cattle or horses. Pa
and the others swallowed the galling insults as the
price they paid for peace.

Jonny fumbled with the lock, thoughts of the outlaws turning his fingers to thumbs. He listened but
there was no sound from inside the barn. Could
this be the night he'd find it empty? He struck the
lock with his fist and the door swung open. He held
up the lantern, but the wavering candlelight only
filled the corners with deeper shadows. His throat
tightened.

"Charlie? You there?" he called hoarsely.

From the far end of the barn came a throaty rumble. The longhorn lumbered up from the straw and ambled into the light. Jonny rubbed his cheek against the sleek head as it nosed his pocket.

"Nothing but cold biscuit tonight," he whispered. "Pa said no more salt until the freighter comes in from Trinidad."

Charlie wasn't particular. Biscuits, pickles, cold beans, anything he could lap his tongue around, was food to his stomach. Jonny grinned as the rough tongue slithered across his palm. He liked the feel of it. For that matter, there wasn't anything he didn't like about Charlie from his sharp hoofs to his velvety stubby horns, from his red hide that rippled gold in the light to the scraggly curl of his tail.

"Can't visit with you tonight, Charlie. Ma's waiting supper."

Picking up the brush, he smoothed the steer's coat with long easy strokes. From long practice the grooming was done quickly. He moved to the cow's stall and hung the lantern on a nail. As he settled himself on the milking stool, Charlie laid his nose across the boy's shoulder.

"Baby," Jonny whispered, shooting a stream of milk into the wide-open mouth. "Silly old baby. What will Mr. Goodnight say when he sees you're still lapping milk?"

Now that the grass was rising, Charles Goodnight would again be trailing his herds up from Texas. Jonny could hardly wait to see his surprise when he looked at Charlie. He'd never believe this was the same starved maverick he'd given Jonny the spring before.

The Goodnight herd had been ready to move north and the three-day-old calf was too young to travel. Instead of shooting him and leaving him to the wolves and coyotes, Mr. Goodnight had carried him across his saddle all the way from the Capulin Vega, down the long Canyon Road, and turned him over to Jonny. Jonny had named him Charlie Texas after Mr. Goodnight.

Those first nights away from the herd had been strange to the little fellow. Jonny had slept close beside him, burrowing into the straw and cuddling the scrawny orphan in his arms to stave off the chill of the mountain wind. He had fed him all the skimmed milk Ma could spare—with frequent additions of pilfered cream. Charlie had grown daily and Jonny delighted in his beauty.

"Jonny! Hurry."

"Coming, Ma."

Dumping an armful of bedding straw, he scattered it with his foot. Then locking the door, he carried the milk and the lantern to the house.

He sniffed hungrily at the crock of baked beans Ma was lifting from the oven. Pa was reading the newspaper and Matt was on his high stool giving Jennie the nightly tussle over his bib. Jonny was glad this wasn't his chore. He'd rather bell a wild plains cow than wrestle with that bib. With his yellow curls and blue eyes Matt looked like the pictures of the angels in the Bible, but the likeness ended there.

"Oh, Matt, don't be so contrary," scolded Jennie. "I haven't got all night."

"You ding-blasted old sidewinder," Matt yelled, clutching the bib with both hands and laughing boisterously.

"Matt." Pa dropped his newspaper and started for the high stool. "You've gone far enough."

Matt dropped his bib and studied Pa's black frown.

"Yes, sir," he said with a smile that sent Pa back to his paper. "I was only playing. You want I should ask the blessing tonight, Pa?"

"It might be a good thing, considering how you've treated your sister," answered Pa, somewhat pacified.

When they were seated at the table Matt bowed his head and folded his hands. The bright curls fell over his shoulders, framing his face in a circle of light.

"Thank you, Lord, for this food. . . .

"Now come on you bawling longhorns and eat these beans or I'll call in the coyotes."

Ma gasped and turned red. Pa half rose from his chair, his eyes blazing. Jonny ducked his head to hide his grin and glanced at Jennie, whose face was in her napkin. Matt leaned back, beaming at them, proud as a preacher after a two-hour sermon.

"I'm about to the end of my rope with that child," Ma said angrily. "Seems whatever I say goes in one ear and out the other. But every word those bull-whackers and freighters say is branded on his mind. Something's got to be done."

Pa stared at Matt as if he were some strange animal dropped on the doorstep.

"I reckon I've been too free in asking the men here," he said apologetically. "They've been so long with cows and mules they forget themselves sometimes."

"I don't begrudge the men their home-cooked meals," said Ma. "There's little enough on the trail to make life pleasant. But it's hard to raise a child in the way he should go, when he hears such talk."

"This ain't anything," volunteered Jonny. "You should hear him at the post when Captain Coe comes in."

Suddenly Ma covered her face with her apron and burst into tears. They all stared, aghast. They had never seen Ma cry before. Jonny squirmed uneasily. Then she already knew about Matt. She had known all the time. He wished he'd cut his tongue out before he blurted out the words. Tattling never helped. It only made a bad mess worse.

Matt leaned over and clutched Ma around the neck, kissing her fiercely through the apron. Pa hurried around the table and patted her awkwardly on the shoulder.

"You're tired tonight, Susan," he said soothingly. "You work too hard. I'll tell the men they can't come any more."

"Work never hurt nobody," Ma answered, wiping her eyes. "It's the worry. And it's not so much the men you invite. It's the one you don't invite."

They all knew who she meant. Pa shrugged helplessly. What was a man to do? Slam the door in Coe's face and turn him against them?

"He's a gentleman when he comes," he said, dropping his hand from her shoulder and going back to his chair. "He likes the children and brings them presents."

"Whose money buys them?" demanded Ma shrilly. "How is a child to know the evil that's in him? Matt fairly worships him. When he's old enough to know the truth, it may be too late."

"Matt's only five," answered Pa.

"As the twig is bent so the tree is inclined. Martin, many a night you've sat at this table and watched Matt with Captain Coe."

"It won't always be like this, Susan," Pa answered patiently, almost pleadingly. "Some day the railroads will cut through the mountains. Then there will be people . . . lots of good people, and courts of justice. Coe and his like will get what's coming to them. Jed Wilson said Coe is a prisoner up at Fort Lyon right now."

"Why didn't you tell me sooner?" cried Ma, her face lighting up like a spring morning. "I wouldn't have made a goose of myself."

She jumped up and began to fill their plates with the food they had forgotten. The corn bread and fried potatoes were cold, but nobody minded. Ma was happy again.

"Now the freighter will come through," said Jennie. "You won't have to worry any more about supplies for the store."

"You think he'll get through tomorrow?" asked Jonny anxiously.

He knew how worried his father had been about the empty shelves. The sugar and dried beans were gone and so were all the mining tools. There was

only a little flour, and the bottom of the salt barrel was showing. The freighter was long overdue.

"I hope he'll come," replied Pa. "My stock's so low I'm ashamed to call the place a trading post."

Ma had made dried peach cobbler, and they all laughed when Matt licked up the last bite with his tongue. Even so, Ma took the dish away and smacked his fingers.

"No more of that, young man. Next time you go without if that's the way you're going to eat it."

Matt looked at her keenly to see if she really meant what she said. He sighed and examined his fingers to see if they were red.

In this short stillness they heard the thud of galloping hoofs along Canyon Road. The sound came

nearer and nearer. They knew when the horse left
the road and turned in the ranch gate. They heard
the creak of leather as the rider dismounted. Then
came a demanding knock that rattled the door
hinges. Fear swept over Jonny as he saw Pa's eyes
lift swiftly to Ma's. For an instant no one moved.
The knock came again, harsh and shattering.

Pa picked up the lamp from the table and walked
to the door. Jonny glanced at the gun rack, hoping
Pa would reach for one. But he didn't. He swung the
door wide and stood with only the light in his hand.

The man outside was tall. He swept off his hat and
smiled. The light shone on his white teeth and his
pale yellow hair. It flickered on his polished boots
and on the big silver belt buckle. It glowed dully on
the gun butt.

The man was William Coe, captain of the raiders
of Robbers' Roost.

2

Two Guns

THERE WAS no sound in the room except for the bubbling of the teakettle and Ma's breath hissing between her teeth. Pa didn't speak. He stood with his hand gripping the door, staring at the man outside who was no longer a prisoner at Fort Lyon.

The outlaw smiled and his hand dropped lightly to his gun. His fingers fondled it, as if he liked the feel of it.

"It's been some time since I stopped," he said, sweeping off his hat and bowing to Ma. "I trust you haven't forgotten me."

Pa laughed and threw back the door.

"William Coe." His friendliness sounded hollow even to Jonny's ears. "I wasn't expecting you. Come in. You're just in time for a bite to eat."

"I've been thinking about Mrs. Hardy's cooking for the last hour."

As Coe stepped in, Jonny was reminded of a half-wild barn cat stalking a chipmunk. Ma hurriedly set another plate and stirred the fire to warm the food. Matt beat his heels against his chair and yelled.

"Captain Coe," he shouted, holding out his arms. "You've come back."

"You little rascal," laughed Coe as he lifted Matt from the chair and held him close. "Here's a man who's always glad to see me."

Matt rubbed his cheek against the outlaw's yellow beard.

"Course I'm glad to see you. We're friends. Did you bring me something?"

"I sure did, partner. Want to guess?"

"No. Give it to me," demanded Matt. "I want it now."

Coe reached into his shirt and brought out a Colt revolver whittled from wood.

"See, it's just like mine," he said, placing his own and the toy gun side by side.

They were alike in every detail—hammer, trigger, and barrel—except that one was dull metal and the other wood.

"Oh, I like it," cried Matt. "Where did you get it?"

"I whittled it out for you while I was in jail—" Coe turned to Pa—"I thought I did a right neat job with only my skinning knife."

He laid a slender-bladed knife on the table. The handle was a deer head of carved ivory. Pa only nodded, and Coe put the knife back.

Matt grabbed the wooden gun and pointed it at Jonny.

"Bang! Bang! You're dead! Bang! Bang!"

"Hush, Matt," said Ma. "You're too noisy."

"Bang! I shot you, Ma."

"Let me see it, Matt," said Jonny. "Please."

"No. You can't have it. He brought it to me. Bang! I shot you, Pa."

Matt began galloping about the room, aiming the gun and shouting, "You're dead! You're dead!"

Pa reached out and caught him by the shirt. Matt laughed wildly and struck his father's hand with the gun barrel. Pa picked him up and carried him, kicking and shouting, into the bedroom. It was some time before he came back alone.

Coe looked up from his plate and laughed.

"You've sure got a little wildcat in that boy. He's the kind the Cimarron country needs. If I had a hundred men with half his spirit, I'd take over the territory."

Pa didn't answer. He looked at his hand where Matt had struck him. It was already turning blue. Jonny glanced quickly at his mother. Her face was harsh as she watched the purple bruise spread across Pa's knuckles.

Now Jonny understood what she was afraid of. All the time he'd been thinking of Matt only as an ornery brat, but it was more than that. It was the way he looked up to Coe, believing that everything the outlaw said was law and gospel. The tales the drovers told of Coe and his raiders were meat and drink to Matt. The wooden gun in his fingers made him as big as any of them.

"How did you get out of jail?" Jonny asked, wondering what cunning trick Coe had used this time. The captain slapped his knee and roared.

"Easiest break I ever made. The soldiers had me there three weeks. All that time I fetched and carried and did their dirty work. By the end of that time I had them all feeling sorry for me. They thought I was innocent as a newborn lamb and all the claims the people had made against me were a pack of lies.

"One day three of my men from the Roost drove in with a load of firewood. Said they were out hunting fresh pasture for a herd of cattle they wanted to summer on the Arkansas. They bought up a wagonload of supplies at the sutler's, and when they drove away I was under the blankets. When we reached an arroyo I crawled out. I got on a horse and headed for Pueblo. The men went back to the Roost with the supplies. I made a pretty good thing out of that Pueblo trip."

He took a small bag from his pocket.

"Met an old prospector. He looked kind of tired and sick, so I just relieved him of his burden. He won't need it any more. Well, thanks for a good meal." He tossed a small gold nugget on the table. "This should take care of it."

A chill ran down Jonny's back as the bit of metal glittered on the checked tablecloth. Dead man's gold. Coe had tossed it out as easily as Pa tossed out lemon drops or tobacco plugs at the post.

"Coe, you're crowding your luck," warned Pa.

Coe laughed confidently and tapped his gun.

"I ride in the shadow of Lady Luck's wings."

Could be the shadow of a cottonwood tree, Jonny thought, angrily. You and your bloody gold and wooden guns. If Matt was only a little bigger, you'd be putting a real one in his hands.

"I'll be on my way," Coe said, pushing back his chair. "Thank you, ma'am, for a delicious meal. I'll be back for another before long." He turned to Pa. "Hardy, my horse is too tired to be ridden farther. I want to be at the Roost by morning, so I'll leave it and take one of yours."

Jonny stood in the door and watched them go to the barn. They were gone only a short time. Coe came back riding Pa's best horse. He stopped in the beam of light cast by the lamp, his long shadow blocking out the light.

"Say, Jonny," he called, "is that good-looking longhorn the half-starved maverick Goodnight dumped on you last spring?"

Jonny nodded. His throat was suddenly too tight for words.

"When you see that drover," Coe went on, "tell him this country ain't big enough for me and him both. I've staked my claim to the Black Mesa country and I don't aim to share it with a lot of Texas longhorns, either two-legged or four-legged."

He started off and his insolent laugh rang through the darkness. The hoofbeats of Martin Hardy's horse grew fainter and fainter and finally died away.

Pa picked up a newspaper and started to read. Ma

sat down beside him and took it out of his hands.

"Martin." Her voice was hardly more than a whisper. "Once when I was a little girl my father took me to a fair. I saw some dolls there. They were made of wood and had strings tied to their hands and feet. The man holding the strings was real clever. He could make those dolls do anything he had a mind to."

"What's wooden dolls got to do with us?" Pa asked gruffly.

"We're like those dolls, Martin. Our hands and feet are tied and Coe pulls the strings. We dance to about any tune he whistles."

"Now, Susan, it ain't that bad," answered Pa. "We've got the ranch, and the trading post is doing well. In another year or two I'll be out of debt. Coe lets the men in this part of the country alone. Leastwise he hasn't robbed or killed any of us. All he asks is food and shelter."

"Maybe he hasn't killed any of us yet," Ma said. "As for robbing, I ain't sure. He's taking your son away right before your eyes. And he's robbed us of our self-respect. When he steps in this house, he's master, not you."

"But he pays."

"Blood money." Ma touched the nugget with the tip of her finger. "Gold from a sick, tired old prospector."

Jonny tiptoed to his room. He couldn't listen any more. Ma was pushing Pa too hard. He was doing what he could without drawing a gun. If it came to that, who could hope to stand up against Coe? Ma didn't understand. She worried too much about Matt. He wasn't much worse than the other little kids in town and as for his cussing, well, Jonny himself cussed like that sometimes just to see how it felt to roll the words on his tongue. But what would happen now that Coe had seen Charlie? Well, if anything happened to that longhorn, someone would pay.

Jonny slipped out of his clothes and climbed into bed. Matt as always, lay sprawled in the middle. As Jonny rolled him over, his hand struck the sharp wooden gun.

3

Doubtful Friendship

JONNY woke several times during the night. Each time he thought of Charlie and wondered if Coe had come back. Once he got up and looked out of the window. In the faint light he could see the barn door was still closed, so he went back to sleep, only to toss and tumble in nightmares of losing his longhorn.

When morning came he was so groggy Ma had to shake him to get his eyes opened. Without waiting for breakfast, he ran to the barn. His heart leaped up when he heard Charlie bawling for something to eat.

He dumped a measure of corn into the feed box. While Charlie ate, Jonny brushed his hide and polished his hoofs. When the last of the corn was lapped up, he turned him into the pasture and watched admiringly as the sun caught the golden lights along the rippling muscles.

Mr. Hardy was cleaning the stalls when Jonny

came back. Matt tagged around underfoot and banged away with his gun.

"What kind of trade did Coe make last night?" asked Jonny. "Did he leave you some old windbroken nag?"

Pa snorted and jabbed the fork into the litter.

"No, I got a real fine horse. Only thing is, it's carrying the Government brand."

"That's a pretty pass," exclaimed Jonny. "What you going to do with it?"

"Give it to the soldiers when they pass this way."

"Then you're out a horse," Jonny pointed out.

"I would have been anyway."

"You could put your own brand on it, Pa," said Matt, sighting down his gun.

"Matt," roared Pa, "if I thought you knew what you're saying, I'd brand your backside with my hand. It beats me where you pick up such talk. I've never yet put my brand on an animal I knew was stolen."

"I hear there's plenty in this country who do," commented Jonny.

"That's no cause for us Hardys to do the same. Looks like your mother was right last night. Someone should make a stand."

"Who's to do it? Who's fast enough?" demanded Jonny.

"Coe gives us no cause to draw," said Pa. "Sometimes I wish he would. His highhanded ways and insults shrivel a man's soul. This Cimarron country used to be a man's country, but now we're all cringing in the shadow of Robbers' Roost, like your mother said."

Jonny ducked his head so as not to see the look in Pa's eyes. Pa was the bravest man he knew . . . braver than Coe, for Pa walked without a gun. He hadn't wanted to trade horses last night. It was the finger tapping the gun that made the trade.

"Don't do it, Pa," pleaded Jonny. "You wouldn't have a ghost of a chance face to face with him."

"Any other way is murder," Pa said quietly. " 'Thou shalt not kill' was a command long before Coe came into the world. No, son, we're men of peace here. We'll wait for the law."

They worked together in silence for a time. Jonny finished the milking while Pa went to the pasture for another saddle horse. He had no wish to ride the one Coe had left.

When breakfast was over, Pa made ready to ride to the trading post.

"Will you need me today?" Jonny asked. "The freighter's likely to come in."

Supplies for the post came down the Santa Fe Trail by way of Trinidad. To Jonny there was no grander sight in all the world than the lumbering Conestoga wagon with its high-stepping mules, the driver cracking his bullwhip, and the waiting crowd hurrahing and throwing their hats in the air. Just thinking about it made his scalp tingle.

"You've still got the corn to put in," Pa reminded

him. "We were going to break the ground along the river. Remember?"

"Suppose the wagon comes," argued Jonny. "You'll need me then."

"I need you worse here," replied Pa. "If the corn makes anything at all, we can get it ground at Maxwell's mill. You know how high freighted-in meal is. The difference would pay off a sizable chunk of debt."

Jonny turned away, his eyes misty with disappointment. He had forgotten the strip of corn ground. But the freighter only came in the spring and again in the fall. Now he'd have to wait all those long months.

He went to the barn and resentfully reached for the harness. He was startled by a commotion from Charlie's stall. Inside he found Matt, crouched in the straw, a rope in one hand and the other hanging onto the legs of the old barn cat and the rooster.

"What in thunderation are you doing?" he roared, snatching the rope.

The cat shot out of the door and the rooster flew into the manger minus his tail feathers.

"Darn you," yelled Matt. "You turned my horses loose."

"Horses!"

"You'd never believe it," said Matt, looking at a long bloody scratch on his arm.

"I bet you're right," replied Jonny. "What's the yarn?"

"I'm a bullwacker. I'm freightin' on the cutoff. Injuns shot my horses. I caught me a couple of wild ones—" he looked seriously at Jonny—"you know those blasted things begin clawing and caterwauling like mountain lions."

Jonny laughed in spite of himself.

"It's a wonder you didn't get your eyes clawed out, you little half-wit. Now hustle into Ma and let her put some turpentine on that scratch before you die of blood poisoning."

"Shucks. I'm going to live forever."

"Git. Before I clout you."

Jonny raised his fist.

"Aw, you wouldn't hit me, would you, Jonny? Not really?" pleaded Matt.

Jonny grinned and dropped his hand. "No, I won't hit you. But get a move on before I change my mind."

Matt galloped out of the barn, spanking himself on the rear and whinnying like a frightened horse.

All week Jonny worked in the field. Charlie's coat suffered, for he was too tired at night to brush him. Matt took over the job, but it was hard for a young one scarcely higher than the steer's nose. Jonny was grateful and didn't throw Matt's gun on the floor when he found it in bed.

Pa left each morning, cantering off briskly, certain the freighter would be in before sundown. When Jonny came in at dusk he didn't have to ask. Pa's horse was already in the barn, and the milking was done.

One night Jed Wilson rode in just at suppertime. Since Coe's escape Jed had been going off, telling no one of his destination, and keeping a mighty close mouth when he got back. Pa had wondered about him, but Jonny only wished he could go with him, no matter where, just to get away from that tarnation plowing.

"Anyone home?" Jed called as he dismounted. "I got news," he shouted as Pa opened the door. "Hardy, the wagon's about six hours out, camped for the night. Should be in around noon tomorrow."

Jed ate with them. Ma celebrated the good news by making an open-face dried peach pie. The sugar was all gone so she sweetened it with blackstrap molasses.

Jonny and his father worked all the next morning cleaning and sweeping the post. Jonny was mixing some adobe to patch a crack in the wall when he heard Lew Black shout. Lew made saddles and boots in a shop fifty yards down the road. When Jonny dashed around the building Lew stood in the middle of the road waving a half-finished boot.

"It's comin'. Freighter's comin'."

Mr. Hardy hurried to the porch and tripped over Jed and Jenk Jarbie, who were sitting with their chairs tilted against the wall taking life easy. They righted themselves and continued to sit. Jenk used to be an old 'Stogie driver himself. Now that he was

married to a widow-woman with property he saw
no cause to get excited.

Heads popped out of doors all up and down the
street. Women stood on their porches shading their
eyes against the glare. Dogs and little boys sprang
up from nowhere. Big boys sprinted down the road
hoping to hop the high-wheeler and ride back in
style. Sam Rogers and his two grown sons ran from
the blacksmith shop, leaving their fire and bellows.

The wagon rolled along the road, dipping into
the arroyos and waddling over rocks. Its bleached
top was dazzling in the thin air. The matched mules
—ten of them—lifted their feet like dancers stepping
off a long-known routine. When the wagon creaked
to a stop Jonny shouted and whistled with the others.

Suddenly he noticed that the wagon top was
splattered with holes. He pointed them out to his
father.

"See you had trouble," Hardy said as the driver
leaped down.

"Yeah. Got held up two . . . three days by high
water, then bogged down in the mud." He wiped
his face with his bandanna and grinned at the crowd.
"Danged if it didn't rain mud-balls."

"Don't look like mud-balls to me," replied Hardy.
"They're bullet holes."

"Oh, them." The driver glanced indifferently at
the top. "Ran into a couple of road agents on t'other
side of the Spanish Peaks. Not much trouble. Joe's
Winchester is mighty convincin'."

The crowd looked with admiration at whiskery Joe and his rifle.

"With Coe in jail the others ain't so hard to handle," he said, as if the matter wasn't worth considering.

"Coe ain't in jail," Jed said. "He escaped."

The driver looked thoughtful; then Joe shook his head.

"It wasn't Coe. He don't waste lead on wagon tops."

He turned to unhitch the mules. Every boy knee-high to a mule's nose rushed up with his hands out, hoping to be the favored one to drive the animals to the livery stable.

"Vamoose," shouted the driver, cracking his whip over their heads, and they scattered like quails.

Mr. Hardy had hired a dozen men and boys to help with the unloading. They leaped into the wagon, the boys grabbing the biggest boxes. They grunted and strained and struggled, till finally they got them into the store. Then they swaggered out, spat on their hands, and climbed into the wagon again.

Little tads darted about like horseflies, getting underfoot and making wild guesses as to what was in the boxes. The men laughed and pushed them aside good-naturedly. One or two became obstreperous and were soundly knuckled. Sam came across one little boy crouched against a wooden bucket marked PEPPERMINTS, his nose wiggling like a hungry puppy's. Sam picked him up and tossed him to Lew.

"Look what they're shipping out of the States now," he shouted.

Lew caught the child and sent him through the air to Jenk. The little boy passed from hand to hand until he landed on top of the cracker barrel inside the store. There he stayed, sucking his thumb, trying to make up his mind whether to laugh or cry.

Jonny felt sorry for him. Sneaking a handful of licorice drops from the candy case, he pushed them into the small fist.

"Here. Chew these for now, Tommy. When Pa opens the peppermints, I'll give you some."

By late afternoon, Pa called it a day and locked the doors.

"Folks will just have to wait until tomorrow if they want anything," he said.

There wasn't much to sell anyway until the stuff was unpacked. Jonny was tired, but he was tired when he plowed, too, and this was more fun.

The best part was yet to come—the unpacking. This would take a long time with Jonny calling out the things in the crates and Pa checking to see if the order had been filled right. The shelves would be full of all kinds of new things to feel and taste and smell.

Going home they passed half a dozen Ute Indian bucks building a fire on the river bank. Mr. Hardy waved and shouted a greeting in the Ute language. Jonny frowned and waved but only because Pa made him.

Every summer the Indians moved into Cimarron Canyon to hunt and fish. The women picked the wild berries and grapes and sand plums. They tanned the hides the men brought in.

Pa said the Indians wouldn't do any harm, but Jonny never liked to turn his back on them. Their eyes always looked as if they were hiding something.

"The Indians are mostly what the whites have made them," Pa explained. "We kill the deer and buffalo and hold them on reservations. Then we expect a few dribbles of flour and beef to make up for what they've lost."

The Indians spent a lot of time in the store bartering for beads, knives, guns, and cooking pots. Pa spent as much time haggling over the hide an Indian brought in as he did with the white trappers. After the trade he always threw in some little extra—a handful of sour drops, a gaudy trinket—just a little something to make the Indian leave happy.

He said it paid off in the long run to have them like the settlers. He tried to get the other white people to go along with him. Most of them did, but a few maintained that the Indians were no better than animals and that a bounty should be paid for their scalps like some of the towns up in Colorado Territory were doing.

It was easier to get along with the Indians than to fight them, Pa argued. A family could get along without a few stolen chickens and a calf or two now and then, but a man with an arrow in his back left a mighty big hole.

At the table that night Pa joked and teased as he hadn't done in weeks. It was hard to eat for laughing. After supper Jennie and Ma cleared the table and washed dishes in a hurry.

"Now," Ma said as she wrung out the dish cloth and dried her hands, "such an occasion as the freighter getting through safe and sound calls for a celebration, something really big, like Matt getting a haircut."

"Ma, you mean it?" he whispered. "Really? Like Jonny's?"

Ma put him back on the high stool and tied her apron around his neck. Matt couldn't sit still. He had to see each clipped curl.

"Hold still, now." She turned a bowl over his head. "I don't want to take an ear."

Matt scarcely breathed as Ma snipped the hair even with the edge. When she lifted the bowl Pa held him up so he could see himself in the little mirror on the washstand.

"Martin," Ma said, "do you think you could find a pair of pants Matt's size at the post? I don't have time to cut down yours or Jonny's old ones."

Matt's eyes were shiny as new-minted dollars as he waited for Pa's answer. He'd never had a pair of store-bought pants. Pa pulled on his pipe and took his time to think the matter over. When Matt was ready to burst with suspense and anxiety, Pa nodded.

Covering his face, Matt crawled under the table.

The others knew he was crying. Matt would fight and roar and swear and not give a plugged nickel who saw him. But let him cry, and he sneaked out of sight like some hurt animal.

"We shouldn't have waited so long," said Ma, half ashamed of herself at being so blind and thoughtless. She laid the shorn curls in the Bible for safe-keeping. "We made a mistake."

"Maybe so," Pa said doubtfully, looking at the little boot sticking out from under the tablecloth. "But he ain't no more than a baby."

"Some babies are big boys when they take their first steps. He's one of them. He's like you, Martin. You're not afraid of man or beast. You're a good man, but you could so easy have gone the other way."

Matt rolled out from under the table and began to strut around the room, showing off his new haircut. The cowlick stood up like the feathers on a fighting cock.

"I'm as big as you are, Jonny," he boasted. "Just wait till I get my store pants. I'll make you run."

He lifted his fists and danced about on his toes. Jonny put up his own fists, and a wild hassle began on the kitchen floor.

"That's enough," Ma said. She carried Matt off to bed. When she came back she closed the door tightly behind her. "Martin," she began, "I hated to spoil the fun, so I didn't tell you sooner. Soldiers stopped today, looking for William Coe."

"I expected them," Pa said without concern. He began removing his boots. "What'd they say?"

"They saw the horse with the Government brand."

"Yeah?"

"They didn't believe me when I said it was Coe made the trade, not you. They think you're letting him pasture stolen stock here."

Pa stopped tugging at his boot and stared at her in amazement.

"You mean they think Pa's in on the rustling?" cried Jonny.

"Looks that way," replied Pa seriously as he tossed his boot in the corner.

4

Still Moccasins

JONNY looked for the Indians on the river bank the next morning, but they were gone. He was relieved, though Indians seemed unimportant beside this new fear the soldiers had laid on him.

Neither Pa nor Ma had mentioned the horse or the soldiers at breakfast. Pa hadn't talked much, and when he did, it was about the new supplies. Soon as everything was unpacked he wanted Ma and Jennie to come in. He always gave them first choice of the dress goods before he put it out for sale. There were some lamps, too, with flowers painted on the chimneys. Ma might like one of them to pretty up the room.

If Pa was worried about the soldiers, he didn't let on. Jonny rode beside him, keeping his fears to himself. There was no use asking. Pa would only tell him to stop worrying over a man's problem. But this wasn't just a man's problem. It belonged to the whole family—to Jennie and Jonny and even Matt.

47

When they reached the post, Jed and the freighters were already sitting on the porch. Martin unlocked the door, then pulled his chair up beside them. Jonny took care of the horses and slipped down beside Pa, his back to the wall and his knees drawn up to his chin.

Pa wouldn't start the unpacking until the freighters had told all the news from beyond. Oftentimes it was so old and haggled by the time it had traveled this far that a man couldn't put much faith in it. Still it was something new and different and touched off hot arguments long after the freighters had gone. Other men in town sauntered over to listen and ask questions.

"How is the South making out since Lee's defeat?" Lew asked. Lew was from Virginia and the Southern cause was close to his heart.

"The Yankees have taken over and are giving the rebels a hard time," answered the freighter. "'Carpet-baggers,' the rebels call them."

"What they doing down there?" Lew yelled. "They licked 'em. What more do they want?"

Then Sam took up the cause of the Yankees, and the war was fought again on the porch of Martin Hardy's trading post.

Jonny yawned and pulled his hat over his eyes. He couldn't understand why they cared. The War Between the States was over and had been for nearly three years. It all happened a long way from Cimarron Canyon.

They'd better save their breath for the soldiers at Fort Union and Fort Lyon. Since those pesky yellow-legs believed Pa was a rustler, they might get the same idea about some others around here who harbored Coe. Pa wasn't the only one.

Jed, too, had lived too long away to care what went on back in the States. Home to Jed was the Shining Mountains and the High Prairies.

"What's goin' on up at Bent's Fort?" he asked when he could make himself heard. "How's the tradin' business with all this talk of railroads goin' through? Don't seem reasonable they'll ever be able to lay tracks through the Rockies."

This was talk Jonny understood and liked. Bent's Fort, up on the Arkansas River, was the biggest trading post west of the Mississippi. It must be next door to heaven, to hear the freighters talk. Store-rooms stacked to the ceiling with all sorts of the finest trade goods in the world. The wagons that left that place threaded the west, tying together the vast new country. They went to Montana and through the green forests of Oregon and across the desert to California, where the blue Pacific washed white sands.

"They've got a pianny up at Bent's Fort," said a freighter. "It sounds mighty purty when one of them good-lookin' ladies plays it."

Once when Pa had taken Jonny to Maxwell's post near Raton, he had seen a piano, but he hadn't ever heard anyone play it. He hadn't dared touch the black and white keys, but it must sound grand. Mr. Maxwell was rich. Folks said he had three of these pianos and his knives and forks were of solid silver.

"Looks like Indians or outlaws would attack Bent's Fort," said Lew.

"It's not so easy as you might think," replied Jed. "Bent's got cannon mounted on all four corners. Gate opens on the river. Bent's nobody's fool."

"That's why he's lasted up there these thirty years," another freighter spoke up. "Even Coe and his gang pass it by."

The talk stopped. Coe was someone they didn't want to think about. The men chewed their tobacco and splattered the dust in silence. Then Jenk stood up and stretched.

"Hardy, my wife said if you had the sugar barrel open, she'd like a pokeful."

"Tell her I ain't found the sugar barrel yet," Martin answered, making no move to look for it.

"Well, I'd better be going," said Lew, squinting at the sun. "Danged if we ain't set the morning away."

"Jonny, go fetch a bucket of fresh water," said Pa. "Put on the coffeepot and don't hold back on the coffee."

"Toss in a horseshoe," called Jed. "If it sinks, the coffee ain't strong enough."

"Don't have a horseshoe," answered Jonny, picking up the water pail. "I'll just toss in the horse."

The well was out of sight behind the store. Jonny lifted the heavy wooden bucket attached to the end of the rope and let it sink into the water. The pulley squeaked as the bucket rose higher and higher. Jonny swung it to the ground and emptied the water into the tin pail. As he set the bucket down he glanced at something sticking out from behind the well curb. His heart thumped in his throat.

It was a pair of dirty moccasins, and the moccasins were on feet. Still feet, with the toes pointed stiffly upward. The water Jonny had spilled ran along the curb and was forming a puddle around them, but still the moccasins didn't move. The Indian must be sound asleep to lie so still.

Jonny set the bucket down and edged along the curb. The Indian lay with his face to the sun, his black hair sweeping across his eyes. His mouth was drawn back showing his strong white teeth. In his chest was a knife with a white deer-head handle.

Jonny turned and ran.

"Pa! Pa!" he yelled, stumbling onto the porch. "Come quick!"

His father caught him by the arm. "Stop yelling and talk," he said, giving him a shake.

"A dead Indian!" Jonny gasped. "Back there!"

The men dashed to the well to see for themselves. Jonny pointed to the knife.

"Pa, look! The knife."

It was the knife Coe had used to whittle out
Matt's gun.

"That don't look like no Indian knife," said one
of the freighters.

The men shifted uneasily, avoiding one another's
eyes. They all knew the knife. Coe had struck in
the Canyon country at last. Not at the white men
who gave him shelter. He had struck where it would
hurt worse. He had killed one of Black Wolf's
warriors.

Jonny's insides trembled. The horse hadn't been
enough. Now here behind Pa's trading post lay a
dead Indian.

"What do you suppose he had against him?" Lew
asked bitterly. "An Indian ain't got nothing worth
stealing."

"What did he have against that man up at Pueblo?" answered Jenk. "He didn't own a cow or a horse to his name. Coe don't need a reason."

"What'll we do, Hardy?"

Jed fumbled for his chewing tobacco. The others waited for Martin to speak.

"Black Wolf will have to be told," he said slowly. "Sam, you and Jed can talk their lingo. You two ride the Canyon and find him. Any of you seen his camp lately?"

"He was camped on Coyote Trail two or three days ago," said Jim. "I seen him when I was huntin' Pa's steers."

"Tell him it's Red Leaf," said Pa as Sam and Jed turned to go.

"Pa, was Red Leaf an important man?" Jonny asked as they started back to the store.

"Any Indian murdered by a white man is important," replied Pa grimly.

Jonny looked back. Only some small boys remained to stare curiously at the dead Indian. The men separated, each going his own way, without looking back.

5

What Price for a Steer

"LEAVE ME be a while, son," Pa said as they went into the store. "We're playing with fire, and Coe has handed us a mighty short stick. Look around and set your hand to whatever needs doing, but leave me be."

Pa settled himself in a chair and put his feet on the counter. Leaning back, he pulled his hat over his face. A stranger might think he was sleeping, but Jonny had seen him work out hard problems before in just this way.

Hunting up a broom, Jonny began on the pack-rat dirt. Adobe walls crack easily, and it was his job to keep them mended. Now the floor was covered with bits of cactus, sticks, shiny buttons, and all sorts of rubbish which the rats had left in trade for the bits they carried away. Jonny swept it into a heap in the middle of the floor and scraped it into a cardboard. As he tossed the trash into the stove he thought he saw the flash of a cartridge.

He dug around in the cold ashes with his fingers, but finding nothing, he decided he had been mistaken.

He dusted the shelves, making them ready for the new merchandise that would soon be unpacked. He straightened the showcases and was just washing the nose prints off the candy-case glass when Sam and Jed came back.

Black Wolf and two of his warriors rode between them. The warriors lifted the dead Indian and carried him away. Black Wolf waited until they were gone; then he came into the trading post. Mr. Hardy stood inside, as one chief waits for another.

Black Wolf wore dirty buckskin leggings and a ragged blue cavalry coat. Around his hips he had tied a white sack on which the word FLOUR was stamped in big red letters. It had once held white flour given to the Indians by the United States Government. The Indians, knowing more about cloth, usually scattered the flour to the winds and wrapped themselves in the sacks.

Black Wolf didn't look fierce or warlike. He was only a sad old Indian with a withered face.

Through the window Jonny saw the men of the town gathering at the roadside. Sam and Jed settled down in chairs near the stove, not because they were cold, but because they wanted to see and hear all that went on.

Mr. Hardy lifted his hand and began to speak. Back and forth went the talk. Jonny, not understanding the language, twisted and squirmed. Jed shook his head and put his finger to his lips. Never taking his eyes off Martin Hardy and Black Wolf, Sam hunted through his pockets for his pipe and tobacco. When he found them, he fumbled through the same pockets for the matches.

"Coe's been inciting the Indians along the Goodnight Trail," he whispered. "He's been telling the Comanches and the Apaches they can take what they want. They struck Goodnight's herd just after he'd delivered the Government's beef at Fort Union. There was a fight. The Comanches drove off a bunch of the cattle and lit out for Mexico."

"Where were the soldiers?" whispered Jonny. "What were they doing?"

Sam shook his head.

"Does Black Wolf know Coe killed Red Leaf?"

"Yes," hissed Jed. "Now pipe down. I can't follow what they're sayin'."

Jonny tried to sit still.

Finding a match at last, Sam lit his pipe. He tossed the match, still burning, into the stove. The trash Jonny had dumped in earlier flamed up and burned furiously.

"Can't understand what they were doing myself," Sam said. "Look, I think the old Indian's softening."

It did look as if Hardy and Black Wolf had come to some sort of agreement. Hardy offered his pipe, filled with his finest tobacco. Black Wolf's face crumpled into a wide smile as his fingers closed around the bowl.

Suddenly a loud blast and flaming flash set the

round lid of the stove dancing. The stovepipe tumbled and rolled across the floor. Black Wolf whooped and roared and started for the door. Clouds of black smoke and soot set them all choking and coughing. Hardy sprang to the door, blocking the way, while Black Wolf yelled and clawed to get out.

"You kill Red Leaf," he shouted. "Now you kill me."

"No, Black Wolf. Listen." Martin Hardy held out his empty hands. "There is no gun."

Then the talk began again. But now Black Wolf was angry. His white friend had tricked him. His friend spoke with the forked tongue of the rattlesnake. There was not truth but poison in his words. He had tried to kill Black Wolf.

Jonny was scared. His tongue, stiff and dry, stuck to the roof of his mouth. He had caused Black Wolf's eyes to glitter with hate. It was all his fault. There *had* been a bullet in the trash. He had tossed it into the stove. Why, oh, why, hadn't he hunted further? Why hadn't he dug until he found the bullet?

Pa's eyes were red with strain and smoke. Sweat burst out on his forehead in big drops, clinging to the soot and smoke. The talk went on and on. Pa was pleading, begging. Black Wolf could have been a stone, so little attention was he paying to Pa.

"What's he saying, Jed?" Jonny whispered desperately, pulling at Jed's sleeve.

"Your pa's got him down to a present. They ain't agreein' on what it's to be."

"Why don't Pa give him what he wants?"

Jed didn't answer and Jonny turned again to Pa and Black Wolf. The Indian must be driving a hard bargain for Pa to hold out so long. What could he want? What meant so much to Pa that he shook his head time after time against that shining hate?

Finally, defeated, Pa turned to Jonny.

"He wants a steer," he said.

"Why don't you give him one?" Jonny was limp with relief. "You've got plenty."

"He wants the best," Pa said. " 'The Golden Chief,' he calls it. He wants Charlie."

"Charlie! No!"

Jonny seized his father's hand.

"Listen, Pa. Tell him you'll give him two or three, whatever he wants. Pa, I'll work for you the rest of my life to pay for them. Honest I will! You'll never have to tell me twice to do a thing. I'll run quick—as soon as you tell me. I'll——"

"You don't understand." Pa's face was as gray as his shirt. "He says we tried to kill him, Chief Black Wolf. Now he will take only the calf which the white man locks so carefully in the barn at night."

"I lock him up because I want him near me," pleaded Jonny. "I like to look at him last thing at night. I want him there when I get up."

"Yes, I know." Suddenly Pa's eyes flashed. He gripped Jonny's shoulder until the pain shot down the boy's arm, numbing his fingers. "I'm begging for peace. If he can't have Charlie, he'll set his warriors upon us. Do I have to plead with you like you were a half-savage Indian? Do you want that longhorn, or do you want a blood war?"

Stunned by the brutal force of his father's words, Jonny's legs grew almost too weak to hold him up. But he couldn't fall. Pa's eyes wouldn't let him. They drew him up. They held him until he was tall and strong.

"I'll get him, Pa." His whisper clanged in his head. "Do I bring him back here, or does Black Wolf go with me?"

"Black Wolf is a chief. Bring the present here. But hurry, son."

Jonny found Charlie feeding at the base of a butte some distance from the road. He whistled and

the big steer lifted his head. He whistled again and Charlie broke into a run. Jonny wheeled in behind him. The long drive began.

Charlie lifted his head, testing the tangy wind from the mountains. He stepped boldly forward, his trim hoofs clicking against the stones. Jonny rode in a daze, a gray mist between him and his red-gold steer. The time may have been long, it may have been short, when he reached the village. He didn't know. He only knew the pain within him was so great his body could hardly hold it.

Jed and Sam, mounted on either side of Black Wolf, waited. They moved in behind Charlie as Jonny turned aside. He flung the reins over the hitching rack and dashed into the trading post, never once looking back. The reins slipped to the ground. His father picked them up and tied the pony.

6

A Branding Party

MARTIN HARDY and Jonny looked around at the well-stocked shelves and at the bales and crates still piled against the walls.

"The store ain't looked so good since I opened it," said Pa. "I'm beholden to you. I couldn't have done it alone."

The place looked good to Jonny too. Pa's words warmed him, for his father didn't praise him often. Most of the time he told Jonny what to do and expected it to be done. This time the work had been different. Pa had given him a free hand in arranging the shelves. Now they looked mighty pretty, filled with brown and blue and pink dress goods and lamps and dishes and bright new pans.

Pa had explained price markings and accounts. He had even let Jonny do a little bartering and trading with the Indians. They didn't know Pa's foot was pressing Jonny's, telling him when to haggle for more and when to ease up and close the deal.

Things had been different at home too. The barn wasn't the same now. In spite of the milk cows and the work horses crunching corn in the lantern light, the barn seemed empty. He and Pa hadn't reached home till long after dark. His arms and back ached from all the lifting he'd done at the store. At night as he stumbled about bedding down the cows with clean straw, his hands did the chores from habit. His mind was too foggy to think about the emptiness.

But once in bed, he couldn't sleep for all he was so tired. The night wind carried the sound of the Indian drums up the canyon. He had to listen to the beat, beat, beat, of those drums. They never stopped. Day and night the drums throbbed. They beat for the corn-planting dances and the hunting dances. And they beat for the white boy's red-gold steer.

"What's the matter with you, son?" Pa shook Jonny's shoulder. "You look like an owl with the sun in its eyes."

Jonny started and grinned sheepishly.

"I guess I was thinking, Pa."

"I hope you was thinking, not just remembering," Pa answered sharply.

Jonny flushed and reached into the candy case for a lemon drop.

"I said you'd earned a little something extra for all you've done," repeated Pa. "How would you like one of those skinning knives? Some mighty handsome ones came in."

"Gosh. You mean any one I want?"

"Take your pick."

Pa turned away and joined Jed and Jenk on the porch. Jonny opened the box and spread the knives along the showcase. He drew in his breath at their sharp beauty, scarce believing that any one of them could be his for the taking. There were knives of every kind and fashion, knives with handles of bone and deerhorn, of ivory and shell and wood. Their slender points could slit a panther's throat if a man was so unlucky as to tangle with one.

Jonny pushed the ivory-handled one aside. It reminded him of another white-handled knife sticking up from a bloody buckskin shirt. The pain of that day came back to him. Pa hadn't scolded about the cartridge in the stove. He had shrugged it off as one of those things that just happen. Bullet or no bullet, the trouble would have come, he said. Coe had riled the Indians, especially some of the young bucks. The killing of Red Leaf was only part of his plan, Pa was sure.

Both Pa and Ma had told Jonny he mustn't punish himself with thoughts of Charlie. The Indians had prowled around and marked the longhorn for their own. They would have managed one way or another. Charlie was as good as gone when the Indians made spring camp in the canyon, so everyone told him. Jonny wouldn't believe the talk. Some way, somehow, he should have saved him. Even if the talk was true, he did not want the white-handled knife. Digging among the other knives, he came up with one of polished abalone shell. The color changed from half-ripe plum to sunflower yellow; the steel blade angled slightly at the end. He tried the edge on his arm, and it shaved the hairs clean as a razor. He carried it to his father.

"Pa, if this one ain't too expensive, I'd be proud to own it."

Mr. Hardy glanced at it with approval.

"Don't think price has anything to do with it this time, son. Take your pick."

"Better make the most of a chance like that," said Jed, reaching for the knife. "They don't come but once."

He took the knife, hefting it, testing it. The point reached beyond his finger tips.

"A knife like this should have a fine sheath," Jed said thoughtfully. "Like the ones the Texas Rangers carry. They make their sheaths out of the tails of buffalo calves. They whittle out a stick just the shape of the blade. Then they kill a calf and peel the tail skin back and remove the bone. After that's done they pull the skin over the stick and leave it till it's dried. They always leave the curly tip hair for decoration. Buffalo calf tails make mighty pretty sheaths."

"You think we could get a buffalo, Jed?" asked Jonny eagerly. "Huh? Do you?"

"Tell you what," said Jed, with a sidelong glance at Hardy. "The buffalo are moving on the plains

now. If your Pa says so, me and you will go hunting one of these days."

Mr. Hardy hesitated, thinking the matter over.

"Pa, I ain't ever shot anything but rabbits and
turkeys and prairie chickens," Jonny pleaded. "I'm
the only man here that ain't got a buffalo."

"Hardy, give the man a chance," Jenk said, winking at Jonny. "He'll die of old age before he gits
that buffalo."

"Where did you have in mind taking the boy?"
asked Hardy.

"Buffalo is thicker'n bees on a honeycomb over in
the Jornada country," replied Jed. "Just on t'other
side of Robbers' Roost."

Jonny gulped. The Jornada! That meant the Cimarron Cutoff of the Santa Fe Trail, right smack in
the middle of the Plains Indians' hunting ground.
And suppose the outlaws didn't want them hunting
about their headquarters. He looked at his knife and
tried to see it in some other kind of sheath, maybe
one of just plain buckskin. But the knife was worthy
of something better. Not even beaded buckskin would
be pretty as that curly buffalo tail.

"I'd have to think that over, Jed," said Hardy.
"He'd be safe as far as Coe was concerned, but if
Coe didn't happen to be there, what about the rest
of the outfit? And the Indians?"

Jed looked hurt.

"I've lived too long as a mountain man and trapper
to be outsmarted by any Cheyenne or Arapaho In-

dian. I've hunted for wagon trains and I've traded with the Indians. Do you think I'd take the boy if I couldn't take care of him? It's time he saw a little something beside this store and the ranch. He's a-growing up ignorant."

Jonny breathed easier. If Jed said there was no danger, there wasn't. Martin Hardy pulled his lip thoughtfully while he looked at Jonny.

"He is shooting up faster than green corn after a rain. I guess I've kept him kind of tied to my shirt tail, so to speak."

"You sure have," Jed said positively. "When I was his age, I'd shot half a dozen bears and more deer'n I could count. My pappy up an' died when I was eight. If I hadn't kept Mammy an' the young 'un in meat, they'd have starved. I've heered you talk how you was turned out to hunt too when you was no bigger'n a chipmunk."

"Times have changed," argued Hardy. "We're civilized now. I want my boy should have things easier than I did. He's better off in the trading post, learning to barter and sell, than traipsing over the country with a gun."

"Oh, Pa!" wailed Jonny. "Do you mean I can't go?"

Jenk got slowly to his feet and walked to the end of the porch. "I hate to interrupt those tear-startin' tales of your childhood," he said, "but somethin' is movin' in on the prairie."

The talk stopped while they watched a streamer

of dust in the sky. Sam sauntered over from the
blacksmith shop, his eyes on the dust, too.

"Can't be cattle," he said. "They're moving too
fast."

The dust rose up in billowing rolls, thinning into
a yellow mist that reached to the horizon.

"Has to be horses," Jenk surmised. "Soldiers, prob'ly,
from Fort Union."

Jonny remembered the horse with the Government
brand in their corral. The nagging fear for Pa edged
again into his mind.

"Soldiers don't show any mercy for their mounts,"
said Jed, spitting tobacco juice a good fifteen feet
in his disapproval. "Looky the way they're pushing
'em."

Gradually the porch filled with curious men who
had noticed the neck-craning and wandered over.
The thunder of hoofs came nearer, and their excitement grew.

The first of the horses swept around the bend.
A rider shot forward attempting to slow the pace
of the leaders. In an instant the herd became a
milling mass of kicking, squealing animals. They were
finally brought to a stop in front of the store. Their
sides heaved, their eyes rolled, and their coats
glistened with sweat. Some had bleeding whiplashes
across their hips. The stench of overheated horses
was sickening.

"I'll be a lily-fingered scalawag if that man on

the big bay ain't Coe," said Jed. "I'd know that brassy rustler if he wore feathers and a breechclout. Looky at him riding over here, cool as a sidewinder rattler."

Jonny stared. It was unbelievable, even for Coe. There were more than a hundred horses and every one of them carried the big US brand of the Government. He must have gotten away with every mount in the garrison.

Coe dismounted and threw the reins to Jonny. "Here, young man, hold my horse!"

Jonny flushed at the insolent sting of his voice. Instinctively, his hands reached for the falling reins and he hated himself when he found the leather in his hands. Why should he hold the horse of a rustler and a murderer? He wanted to throw the reins back into Coe's face. He wanted to scream at him to hold his own stolen horse. What right had he to order decent people around like they were cattle? The right of the gun was all. He lifted his arm, but Pa's grip on his shoulder steadied him. The tenseness of the men compelled him to hold his tongue, forced him to grit his teeth, to hang onto the sweat-lathered horse.

"You two"—Coe pointed to Sam and Lew with his whip handle—"build a fire! I'm asking all my friends to a branding party. I'm the best hand with

a running iron in the territories. When I'm through, anyone who wants a good horse at a reasonable price can step right up. Now get the fire going and bring out the irons!"

"The brassy fool," muttered Jed. "He ought to know who's best. He's had enough practice changin' honest brands."

They all watched grimly as Sam and Lew returned with a bucketful of coals and a handful of hot irons. Coe and his raiders took the irons and began to cross out the US brand.

"Now they belong to the Double Cross outfit," laughed Coe, and his men roared at the joke.

"Mark my words, son," said Martin. "Law and order will come to the Cimarron valley. Coe and his men are riding high now, but it won't always be like this."

"It's the truth, so help me," said Jed fervently.

Jonny turned from them to the surging mass of horses. Who would raise a hand against Coe? The few who had tried to protect their own hadn't lived long enough to tell what happened. These men in town were peaceful men. They didn't wear guns. They lived and let live. They bore Coe's ruthless insults rather than carry the mark of murderer.

Maybe it was best so, he reasoned. These men were not cowards. They had traveled the Jornada —the Journey. That one word held all the terrors of the overland trails. The waterless miles, the parched grass that turned to powder on the tongues of thirst-

maddened cattle, the Indian attacks, and the flaming
wagons. No, they were not cowards, these men. They
had traveled the Jornada.

They were men with families, like Pa. What would
happen to Ma and Jennie and little Matt if Pa chal-
lenged Coe? The Cimarron country was hard on
women and children, even with a man at their sides.
Jonny's knees grew weak as water. He wiped his
wet face on his sleeve.

Let Coe come. Let him strut and boast and bully.
The price was cheap enough for life. His father's
fingers dug into his shoulder, and Jonny squirmed
away from his grasp.

"I sure feel for them horses," said Jed. "Coe will
sell them in a day or two. Someone else will slap
on another 'hot iron' before this brand has healed.
Then the soldiers will find them, and back goes
the old US."

Martin nodded. "Coe and the Indians keep this
country pretty well stripped of horseflesh," he said.
"But he's riding with a rope around his neck, and
it's a lonesome ride."

Coe struck the last brand and threw the irons
aside. Sam gathered them up and hurried into the
forge out of sight. The scent of burnt hair and
seared flesh hung heavy in the air. Coe looked up
at Martin and Jonny and waved his hat. Jed turned
away.

"Hey, Jonny, want to earn a dollar?" Coe called.

"Help take these horses across the river while I snatch a bite to eat at the tavern."

"Jonny's Ma wants him right away," said Martin, giving him a shove toward the door.

Coe flushed and Jonny's spine chilled.

"Just thought the boy could use a dollar," Coe said. "It's good money."

"Gosh, Pa!" said Jonny as the door closed behind them. "A dollar! He sure is a free spender."

"His kind have to spend their money free and fast," replied his father angrily. "They don't have much time to enjoy it."

7

Doubting Soldiers

THE CAVALRYMEN came the next day. There was no mistaking their dark blue coats and light trousers with the yellow stripe down the legs as they rode over the brow of the hill. Jonny ducked his head and began chopping weeds with all his might, hoping they would ride past if he pretended not to see them. There wasn't anything he could say about the horse that his mother had not already said. They wouldn't be likely to take his word if they hadn't believed her.

The soldiers drew up by the side of the field and talked together. Finally one of them called.

"Hey, boy. Come here!"

Jonny laid down his hoe and started toward them. He took his time picking his way through the green corn tips.

"What's your name?" demanded the sergeant.

"Jonathan Hardy, sir."

The sergeant smiled knowingly and nodded to his

75

men. "I'll do the talking." Then turning to Jonny, he said, "We're from Fort Union. We have reason to believe the outlaw Coe stops at your place."

"That's right," answered Jonny. "He does sometimes."

The sergeant blinked in surprise. This was certainly not the answer he had expected.

"Has he been here, lately?"

"Yes, sir."

"When?"

"Last week. Might have been the first of this week," said Jonny carelessly. "I don't remember exactly."

"What did he stop for?"

"What he always stops for—Ma's cooking."

"Sounds like a good enough reason," put in one of the soldiers, winking at Jonny.

The sergeant frowned, but the wink eased Jonny's tenseness.

"Did Coe give your father a horse?" demanded the sergeant accusingly.

"No, sir. He left his own horse and took one of Pa's."

"It amounts to the same thing," said the sergeant with a shrug.

"Not by a long shot, it don't," exclaimed Jonny. "Coe didn't ask. He just took Pa's horse and left a stolen one in its place. You know that. My mother told you."

The sergeant looked at him coolly.

"I know what your mother said. Now I want to know what you say. Seems like your father's mighty free and careless with his horses."

Jonny bristled angrily at the sergeant's taunt.

"Not so careless as you fellows at Fort Union," he said defensively. "We only lost one. You lost a garrisonful."

"What do you know about those horses?" shouted the sergeant. "Where are they?"

"Last I saw, Coe was heading toward the Roost,"

replied Jonny, pointing toward the east. "They're probably scattered from here to yonder by now. Lots of folks don't ask questions about brands. Not when Coe is selling horses, they don't."

The sergeant frowned as he looked out across the red sandstone hills. They were threaded by trails that crisscrossed and meandered until only the deer and the bobcats—and the outlaws—knew their way about.

"I take it Coe's no friend of yours," said one of the soldiers kindly.

"Coe hasn't got a friend," Jonny answered bitterly. "We're all just afraid to say we're his enemy."

He turned away, feeling he'd been disloyal to his father and to all the others who hated Coe but endured his insults for the sake of peace. Suddenly he remembered something and came back.

"I'm curious about those Fort Union horses," he said. "You got all fired up about Pa's one horse. How come you yellow-legs let Coe get away with all yours?"

The men grinned sheepishly, while the sergeant brushed specks of dust from his trousers and said nothing.

"Go on, Sarge," urged a soldier. "You're doing the talking here."

The sergeant started to ride away, but the roars of laughter from the men stopped him.

"I can't see the army's business is any concern of this boy," he said, glaring at Jonny.

"I think it is. You've practically accused his father of throwing in with Coe." The soldier grinned at the sergeant's discomfort. "It happened this way, Jonathan. Our commander is new to the west. When three good-looking, well-dressed men rode up to the fort with a hard-luck story about being robbed, he fell for it. He hired them to bring in wood and do some of the dirty work around the corral. Seems he hired a famous outlaw, one William Coe by name, and a couple of his gentlemen of the road. Next thing we knew they'd driven off every riding horse we had. Now we're out looking for him and trying to buy more horses."

"A most regrettable occurrence," added the sergeant stiffly.

The soldiers laughed. To them it was a huge joke on the new commander and this pink-cheeked sergeant who was taking it so to heart.

It wasn't funny to Jonny. Their laughter made him see red. They could twiddle their thumbs while Coe ran off with their horses and it was a most regrettable occurrence. But let a man be forced, practically at gun point, to trade one horse and he was hunted along with the thief.

"You soldiers got brass coming around here and insulting folks," he blazed out. "The soldiers up at Fort Lyon had him behind bars and let him escape. You men down at Fort Union ain't any better. Pa says to wait for the law. What law? People around here are beginning to wonder what side of the law the army's on."

Jonny was frightened at his own boldness. He began to tremble, but he couldn't seem to stop. His pent-up fear and hate made him toss caution to the winds. The words weren't his own but those he'd heard all winter around the stove in the trading post. They were the words of the trail drivers and cattlemen who had lost their herds, of the ranchers and farmers and the post riders who had all suffered losses. He'd heard the same talk when Red Leaf was killed and Black Wolf rode away with Charlie. The citizens of the canyon country had a right to expect help from the army and they weren't getting it.

"What were you doing when the Comanches attacked the Goodnight herd?" Jonny went on wildly. "Black Wolf said the drovers begged for help."

"We couldn't go," explained the sergeant. "By the time we got word, our horses were gone."

"You played into Coe's hand," cried Jonny in disgust. "He was there to stir up the Indians. He took your horses and left you cooling your heels in the blockhouse."

"We know that now." The sergeant was almost humble. "I shouldn't have spoken so hastily about your father. I'm sorry."

"The sergeant's new to the territories, Jonathan," explained one of the soldiers. "But he's learning. One of these days he'll find out what you people are up against."

"Thanks, Jonathan," said the sergeant, holding out his hand. "I don't often get told so straight. Perhaps the next time we meet, you'll know which side of the law we're on."

Jonny shook hands, bewildered at the sudden show of friendliness.

"I guess I've talked too much," he said, overcome with embarrassment. "I hope you don't hold it against my pa."

"I won't. You've changed the look of things." The sergeant touched his hat. "Good-by, Jonathan. I promise you, this time when we take Coe, he'll get the justice he deserves."

Jonny felt a swift pity for the soldiers as they disappeared around a hill. No one knew how many men Coe had under his command, but it was common talk there were more renegades than soldiers in the territories.

And Coe was nobody's fool. His plans moved like clockwork, or someone answered for the mistake. Red Leaf could have been that unlucky person. He could have told Black Wolf of the Comanche raid before it had actually taken place. He could have threatened to tell Pa.

With Goodnight racing toward Mexico after his vanishing cattle and Pa with Red Leaf's murder on his hands, Coe would have no trouble over the army's horses. The ease with which his plans worked out made him bold and confident. He would flaunt his cleverness in the faces of the very men who gave him shelter. It would only drive their fear of him deeper and tighten his hold upon them. If any man held hidden thoughts of turning him over to the army, the theft of the horses only proved how puny the army really was. Coe was the law in the Cimarron country. He wanted no mistake about that.

In the following days the soldiers searched the hills and plains. They picked up Coe's trail at several ranches where he had tried to sell horses. They bought back several of their own from men who found it profitable—or necessary—to trade with Coe. He left a well-marked trail, but the outlaw himself was as elusive as a shadow. He was always just beyond.

The soldiers rode in and out of town, stopping often to talk with Martin Hardy. Sometimes he went with them. Hardly a day passed without some of them stopping at the ranch house. Mrs. Hardy mothered them all and sent them away with mended shirts and full stomachs. They repaid her by doing chores about the place. They mended the barn door when the wind broke the hinges. They chopped wood and stacked it beside the kitchen door. They carried interminable buckets of water.

Mrs. Hardy didn't complain about the extra work. The potatoes and beans and corn bread they ate were her payment for peace of mind. Coe wouldn't be likely to visit them while the soldiers were around.

8

Charles Goodnight

ONE MORNING Pa handed Matt a basket of seed
corn and told him to go to the field with
Jonny.

"What'll I do with him down there?" Jonny grum-
bled. "I'll be chasing after him all over the place."

"A little work might take some of the ginger out
of him," replied Pa. "Besides, he hears too much and
talks too much around the soldiers."

"Oh—" Jonny glanced quickly at Matt—"little pitchers."

"With big ears. That's me," said Matt, grinning
impudently.

"And a lot of lip," added Jonny. He shouldered
the hoe and started down the path. If Matt's tall
tales of rustlers were putting ideas into the soldiers'
heads, it was time someone got him out of the way.
"Come on, runt. Corn don't plant itself."

So Matt went to work dropping seeds in the holes
while Jonny covered and tamped down the soil.

After the corn was in, Ma decided to give the bunk-house its spring cleaning. With warm weather upon them, not many travelers wanted the shelter of a roof. They preferred the ground under them, with the starry sky above.

The two boys carried water and scrubbed the floor with strong lye soap. They lugged out the mattresses and emptied out the old straw. Ma washed the ticks and spread them in the sun to dry. Then Jonny and Matt filled them with prairie hay and put them back on the beds.

Ma took to singing as she worked, something she hadn't done for months. Catching Jonny's eyes on her, she broke off in the middle of a high trill and laughed.

"You'd think I was too old to be carrying on like this," she said. "But with the soldiers coming and going, seems like I've turned my troubles over to them."

Jonny felt freer himself since the soldiers understood about the horse. They had taken it away and nothing more was said.

One night Pa brought word that the Goodnight cattle had reached the Vega.

"Do you suppose Coe will make good his threat against him?" Jonny asked as they were doing the chores.

"Charles Goodnight can take care of himself," answered Pa. "Son, quit worrying your head with men's problems. Bed down the cows and come in."

Picking up the milk pails, Pa went to the house. Jonny swung the pitchfork in silent fury. Sometimes Pa talked like he was no bigger than Matt. He wished he knew where men's problems began and boys' left off. One day he was doing a man's work, and the next they treated him like he didn't have enough sense to pound sand in a rat hole.

He went into Charlie's empty stall. Times like this he missed his longhorn. He couldn't remember worrying much when Charlie was here. His going had left an emptiness that had to be filled, but the thoughts that rushed in to take his place were forbidden. Men's problems, so Pa said. Too big for a boy to bother with. But Mr. Goodnight was a boy's friend, and Coe was a boy's enemy. What that outlaw did to him and Pa and Ma—yes, Black Wolf too —he did to Jonny.

Jonny threw himself down on the clean hay in the stall. He wished he could turn back time and hold it fast, with him and Charlie together again.

The next day Mr. Goodnight came home with Pa, and they heard the rest of the story of the Comanche raid.

"We'd just delivered the five hundred head of cattle the Government had ordered to Fort Union. The wily boogers were smart enough to wait for that. They knew most of them cows went to their own people on the reservation. Next night they stampeded the herd. We sent word to the fort, but the same night Coe'd made off with their horses. He'd left five old wind-broken nags not fit to carry a saddle, let alone a man too. There was nothing to do then but go after them ourselves.

"I took ten men and started. The Comanches were headed for Mexico with seven hundred head. They traveled fast, crowding the cows to the limit. We came across cattle they'd killed because they couldn't hold the pace."

"Why did they kill them?" asked Jonny. "They could pick 'em up later."

"They knew we'd be right behind them," explained Mr. Goodnight. "They didn't want us to gather 'em.

The second night we caught up with them. There were about fifty Indians in the raiding party. We fired on them and they returned the fire. We lost three men. We didn't have a ghost of a chance. But we could've licked 'em if we'd had help from the fort."

"It's discouraging," said Pa bitterly. "Seems everything that happens around here points to Coe."

"Looks that way," responded Mr. Goodnight. "Things are too well timed."

"Mr. Goodnight," said Jonny hesitantly, "I don't know whether I should speak up or not, but I think you ought to know. Coe's been making threats he's out to get you. He said these prairies ain't big enough for you and him both."

"That so?" Mr. Goodnight calmly bit off a chew of tobacco. "In that case, I'll stay out of his way."

"You'll what? You mean you'll let him get by with such talk?"

Jonny's disappointment showed in his face. Mr. Goodnight had been an army scout in Texas. He had taken part in more Indian fights than he could count. It didn't seem possible such a man wouldn't track down Coe to his hideout and make him prove his boasts.

"Sometimes it takes more courage to stay away from your enemy than to go after him," Ma said with an understanding smile.

"You never said a truer word," replied Pa fervently. Jonny mulled these thoughts around in his mind.

He remembered the look on Sam's face the day he
carried the coals and hot irons so Coe could change
the Government brands on the horses. Sam could
have killed the outlaw from the blacksmith shop
easy as not. They'd have been rid of him. But that
wouldn't have been the end. Coe's men would have
opened fire. No telling who would have lain in the
road when it was all over. It was just possible Jonny
himself wouldn't be here now, listening to that
mocker splitting his throat in the piñon tree, if Sam
had used a gun that day.

"I've got no time to waste on an outlaw," continued Mr. Goodnight. "Too many people are depending on me. The war ruined the Texas ranchers.
They came home to find their fences and houses
falling down. Their herds have grown so big the
land can't feed them. But them cattle ain't worth
the hides on their backs until they get to market.
I'm trying to get 'em to Denver. If I have to face
Coe, I will, but I'm not going out of my way just
to prove who's biggest."

Then the puzzle pieces began falling in place for
Jonny. Just like Sam holding back to save the town,
so Mr. Goodnight would do the same for the ruined
ranchers in Texas.

"Have you tried trailing through Indian country
into Kansas?" asked Martin.

Mr. Goodnight snorted in disgust.

"Once. But those pigheaded farmers met us at
the line with guns. Texas cattle ain't popular in

Kansas. They say our cows carry Texas fever and they don't want their herds infected. Biggest piece of tommyrot I ever listened to. It's fight farmers or Indians no matter which way we trail. And always there's thieves and rustlers. If it ain't Coe, it's some of his kind."

They sat still, thinking over what Mr. Goodnight had said. The mockingbird sang on. The moon was high, washing the hills in white light. The Indian drums were quiet. Tonight this little corner was a peaceful place, but each knew that trouble lay only as far away as the raiders of Robbers' Roost.

"Well, I've run on like a gabby woman," said Mr. Goodnight at last. "Almost forgot what I came for. Martin, we lost our provender in the Comanche raid. You think you could get a load of corn and flour through the canyon? Say by the end of the week?"

Martin thought a minute, silently running over the problems such a trip would entail.

"I think I can," he answered. "Likely there's someone in town who will drive the wagon through."

"I'd take it as a favor." Mr. Goodnight threw his saddle and blanket under the cottonwood tree. "See you in the morning."

"Pa, let me take the wagon through," said Jonny eagerly as he followed his father into the house.

Ma turned on him sharply. "That's mighty big talk for a young one. I want no more of it."

Pa laughed and roughed Jonny's hair the way he

did Matt's when the little boy was mouthy. Jonny jerked away.

"A tad like you! Sounds like someone's getting too big for his britches."

"Tad?" shouted Jonny. "I ain't a tad when it comes to plowing and planting corn and hoeing till my back breaks. I can fetch and carry at the post all day right along with the men. Now, when a chance like this comes along, I'm nothing but a tad. It ain't fair, I tell you. It ain't fair."

Ma laid Matt on the cot and pulled off his boots.

"That will do, young man," she said to Jonny. "You'll not take one step down the Canyon Road by yourself."

"But it's only to the Vega," argued Jonny. "Not more'n fifteen miles."

Matt opened his eyes. "Shut up. You're yelling me awake. That's Captain Coe's road. He don't want you riding on it."

"Shut up yourself." Tears of exasperation and rage filled Jonny's eyes. "I've got as much right on the Canyon Road as he has."

"Right or no right, it's Robbers' Roost country." Ma's voice said plainly she didn't want to hear any more about it. "Martin, it's time you took Jonny in hand."

"He'll be all right in the morning," Pa said. "Son, what would you do if the Indians decided they wanted the corn? Or maybe some of Coe's men stopped you?"

Jonny stamped off to bed, not bothering to answer. Coe owed him a favor or two, considering all the insults he'd had to swallow from him. As for the Indians, they had his yearling. That ought to satisfy them. But he knew a steer eaten days before wouldn't mean anything to the Indians. A load of corn would be mighty tempting. Jonny's toes curled uneasily under the blanket. He didn't know whether to be glad or mad that Pa wouldn't let him go.

9

Down the Canyon Trail

EARLY the next morning Jonny began to load the wagon with corn. Mr. Hardy helped for an hour or two before he left for the trading post. By mid-afternoon the load was shaping up. Jonny was getting an obstinate satisfaction out of doing a man's job well, even though his britches were little and Pa gave him no credit.

He was just topping off the wagon when Jed Wilson rode in, followed by Martin's pack horse already loaded with supplies for the Goodnight camp. Jed wore his holsters and carried his old Sharps rifle.

"Come on, Jonny," he called. "We're off to the Capulin Vega."

"I ain't," Jonny grunted. "Pa said I couldn't go."

"He changed his mind," Jed said with a wheezy laugh. "He hired me to ride guard, then couldn't find a driver. Kind of think he had you in mind all the time. He didn't look very hard."

"You mean it?"

"Oh, he didn't give in without a struggle." Jed snickered and shot a jet of tobacco juice over the wagon. "He thinks I'm too old and you're too young, but takin' us together we make one good man. And that ain't all." Jed leaned over the saddle horn and lowered his voice. "After we leave the provisions at the camp, you and me is goin' huntin'."

"Jed, you ain't joshing me," pleaded Jonny, ready to bawl if Jed was lying. "You wouldn't be just telling me that?"

"True as gospel," replied Jed. "Go tell your ma and gather up your gear."

Jonny tore to the house, leaping like a mountain goat all the way. He began yelling for Ma before he reached the door. She rushed out, tripping over Matt, who managed to get there ahead of her. She couldn't make heads or tails of what Jonny was trying to tell her, so she finally called in Jed.

"I don't like it," she said, frowning at Jed as if he was at the bottom of this sudden change of Martin's mind. "But if his father says he can go, I haven't anything to say."

Jonny rushed for his gun and cartridges. His mother rolled his banket and took a tin cup and plate and a big horn spoon from the shelf. Then she set them down to the table.

"At least you start off full," she said sourly. "Likely you'll be coming back hungrier than a winter-starved wolf."

Jed looked at her with hurt dignity.

"Ma'am, I'm sure you mean no offense, but I've took care of myself in the wilderness for nigh onto fifty years. It ain't likely we'll go hungry on a piddlin' little huntin' trip like this."

Mrs. Hardy tried to smile as she filled his coffee cup again.

"Don't mind me, Jed. His father knows how I feel about that part of the country. Jonny ain't never spent a night away from home. I'll worry till he's back safe."

"Oh, Ma, don't take on so," said Jonny, red to his ears. "Jed'll think I'm a baby and won't take me."

"Nothing would please me more," snapped his mother. "Jed, I could take trouble with the Indians. They're what God made them. But that nest of evil at Robbers' Roost—it don't seem right to let a young one go near, even with a brave man like you."

Jed, somewhat mollified by this acceptance of his courage, wiped his mustache on his sleeve. Jonny leaped up, knocking his chair across the room.

"Young one! You call me a young one! I'll be thirteen in another week," he blazed out. "If it was Matt screaming and yelling to go, you'd say you'd kept him a baby too long. What are you doing to me? I fetch and I carry and I lug and I tote. And my own ma calls me a baby."

His mother turned on him sharply.

"Hush. You was the one used the word. There's no call for such talk. Go pack your gear." She turned to Jed as Jonny rushed headlong out of the room.

"What's got into the boy? He ain't willful and head-strong like Matt. Leastwise he hasn't been till now."

"Nothin's wrong but growin' pains, ma'am," Jed said kindly.

"He'd better grow with less noise then," Ma answered meaningfully.

Jonny lugged his gear to the wagon and made a place for it beneath his feet. Saddling his pony, he tied him to the end gate along with the pack horse. He hopped up to the seat and laid his rifle beside him. At the last minute his mother came running out with a flour sack.

"Here's some victuals," she said, tucking the bag securely at his feet.

"We'll meat ourselves," Jonny answered gruffly.

"Have a good time," she answered, paying no mind to his surliness.

"Ready?" Jed called. "Much obliged for the grub, ma'am."

Jonny grabbed the lines and yelled to the team. He followed Jed down the Canyon Road without looking back.

The road narrowed as it swung around the sharp foot of a monstrous rock. Jed went ahead, keeping a sharp lookout. There were only the familiar many-colored hills and glittering rocks. Chipmunks scuttled under stones and chaparral cocks streaked across the sand, frightened at their passing. The road was rough, cut by arroyos and dry creek beds, carrying the constant threat of flash floods from the mountains.

Jonny joggled about on the high seat, feeling very much a man. The miles inched behind them. The sun hung low in the sky. They dipped into a valley, and Jed held up his hand. In the shadows lay Black Wolf's camp. Women and children clustered about the glowing fires. Lean dogs sniffed about, licking dried bones. A few magpies hovered at the rim of darkness.

"I don't see any bucks about," said Jed. "But that ain't no sign."

"They didn't beat the drums last night," said Jonny. "I remember listening when I went to bed. I always hear them because . . . well, you know—they took Charlie."

"The men must be off hunting," went on Jed, ignoring the reference to Jonny's longhorn. "But the

women can smell a load of corn farther than they can a skunk. Touch up the horses a might. There's a good camp site up the road a piece."

Jonny slapped the reins, and the horses quickened their pace. His bones ached from all the corn lifting and the long stretch on the hard wagon seat. The Indians wouldn't be likely to make a show of force, but they could move like shadows. He and Jed would have to make camp far enough away to discourage a night visit. There was no use starting a brawl that might lead to something worse. Red Leaf's death was too fresh in Jonny's mind to risk a repeat.

The wheels dipped into a rocky stream bed. The horses lowered their heads and sucked in the cool water. Jonny's throat was parched from the dust and the heat. Watching the horses, he gulped, thinking how good it would feel to have water sliding down his throat.

"We'll follow up the creek a hundred yards or so," said Jed. "It's shallow with a rock bottom. The water will cover our trail."

Jonny looked back. The hill shut away the light from the Indians' fires.

"You think the Indians will follow this far?" he asked.

"They ain't the only scalawags ridin' at night," replied Jed. "We'd be settin' ducks for anyone that came along if we camped by the road."

Jonny turned the team up the creek, following Jed

more by sound than sight. At last Jed caught a bridle and led the team up a gentle slope to a towering pile of rocks. He swung stiffly from the saddle.

"We'd best not let the horses forage tonight," he said. "Tie them to the wheel and give them a bait of corn."

Jonny jumped down and began to follow Jed's orders. The older man built a fire where it was hidden by a rocky cliff.

Jed's hot coffee and Ma's unasked-for leftovers took some of the weariness from their bodies. Jonny leaned against the cliff, looking at Jed's lean, wrinkled face and the cowhorn mustache. His neck was scrawny as a tom turkey's at molting time. His sharp Adam's apple moved with every gulp of coffee. No one could ever call Jed handsome, but there was a patient kindness to his face that satisfied Jonny.

A wolf howled and Jonny's scalp prickled as the lone wail echoed among the hills. He snuggled closer to the fire.

"Good idea to keep the fire going tonight," suggested Jed. "Wolves and bears won't bother us, but there's mountain lions in these rocks. They ain't likely to attack people, but them cats sure like horse flesh."

"I'll take first watch," said Jonny, hoping Jed didn't hear the quaver in his voice.

"No need," answered Jed, gnawing off a bite of tobacco. "I sleep with one eye and both ears open. Git your rest. We've a long day ahead."

Jonny rolled over and pulled the blanket against his neck, shutting out the cold mountain wind. He woke once during the night to find Jed sitting up and looking off into the darkness.

"Anything the matter?" he whispered.

"Horses' hoofs across the creek."

"Many?"

"Don't know how many, but 'twas more'n a few," Jed whispered.

"You think it's Coe with the Government horses?"

"Ain't likely. Coe turns his rustlin' into cash quick as he can. Whoever was trailin' them wasn't curious. They couldn't help seein' our fire."

"Indians?"

"Them boogers is too lazy to travel by night, lessen they're up to some devilment."

"Wonder who it was," said Jonny.

"A man lives longer around here if he don't have no curiosity," answered Jed. "We got all the business we can tend to, and maybe more."

The next morning Jonny waded across the creek and looked for tracks, but evidently the horses had been farther away than he thought, and the clear night air had amplified the sound.

"Hustle with the horses," Jed called. "They've been fed."

"What about us?" asked Jonny. "Don't we eat?"

"We ain't horses, so we don't get none," answered Jed, with a grin kinder than his words. "Look at the clouds over the mountains. They've got the makin's of flash floods, Jonny. The trail ahead has got some

bad arroyos. We could be held up hours waitin'
for the water to run off."

Jonny backed the team to the wagon and tried
not to think of his lean stomach. Horses came first,
he knew, but it didn't keep him from thinking of
crisp salt pork and hot coffee.

"Put this in your mouth," said Jed. "It's a piece
of prickly pear, peeled smooth and clean."

"Do I eat it?" Jonny asked doubtfully.

"Suck it. It keeps your mouth moist and makes
you forget you're hungry. I sucked them things many
a time when I was bullwhacking on the Jornada."

The cactus didn't taste like much. It certainly
didn't take away the emptiness, but Jed said to suck
it, so Jonny did.

"Git the wheels rollin'," Jed called as he swung
into the saddle. "Wagon, ho-o."

Jonny grinned and a shiver of excitement chased
up his spine. One wagon and a few horses weren't
much of a train, but the trail was ahead. He cracked
his whip and braced his feet as the wagon dropped
into the creek.

In the pale dawn the rocky stream lost some of
last night's dread. Little fish skittered along the
shallows and red-winged blackbirds darted up from
the reeds.

"Well, that's behind us," Jed said as the wagon
lurched onto the trail.

"It wasn't so bad," Jonny said confidently. "It
could have been worse."

"Look at them hills," Jed said, pointing to the

peaks now lost in storm clouds. "They're a-breedin' flash floods right now, and don't you forget it. These pretty little streams is treacherous, that's what they are. Treacherous, do you hear?"

Jonny had forgotten. All his life he'd heard of flash floods that swept away unwary travelers. But it always happened to some stranger, some person ignorant of the ways of nature on the high prairies. Likely that was one thing Pa meant when he said there was more in the canyon than met the eye. Jonny guessed he'd done a lot of talking he'd best keep to himself. Would he have known to make camp away from the trail, or if he had, would he have known where to lie hidden? He doubted it. And who were the riders who passed in the night? Suppose they'd been curious and investigated their camp. What would he have done? He'd been so sleepy when he rolled in he'd forgotten to take his rifle from the wagon.

It was mid-morning before Jed decided to stop for breakfast. Jonny's stomach had been grumbling for the last hour. He'd broken off a handful of corn kernels. Corn kept horses alive and he figured he'd live on it, too, until Jed called a halt.

They drew aside from the trail and Jonny built a fire. Jed made coffee and fried strips of salt pork. In the valley below, a herd of antelope was grazing. Jonny wanted to try for one, but Jed wouldn't let him. There wasn't time, he said, if they were going to reach the Vega by sundown.

The food lifted Jonny's spirits, but he knew they'd have gone higher if only he'd had antelope steaks. He'd never killed an antelope. He'd settle for one on this trip if he couldn't get a buffalo. Besides, antelope hide might make a good sheath for his knife.

The road twisted on, following the winding Cimarron. Sometimes the hills crowded close to the river, then the road clung to the rocks, staying away from the loose sand. Again the hills swung back, forming valleys rich in buffalo grass, with an occasional juniper tree or a dwarf cedar. Trails led back from the river, showing deer and bear and other wild animals watered there.

Late in the afternoon they sighted Capulin Mountain. It reared against the sky like an overturned bowl with the bottom cracked out. Scrub cedars covered the steep slopes. The Vega—the vast grazing land—lay all about them.

The road had been gradually rising all the afternoon and the plodding horses strained against the wagon. The wide sweeps of slow-rising hills lay lush with grass. Shadows of deeper green marked the water sinks and stream beds.

"The Goodnight herd should be just beyond old Capulin," said Jed. "I'll be mighty glad to turn this load over to Charlie. A man's life is cheap with a haul like this."

"Shucks," Jonny said. "Nobody bothered us."

"Luck, pure luck," replied Jed. "We ain't there yet. Now what do you suppose them customers want?"

Jonny turned in surprise. He hadn't heard the three horsemen coming up behind them. They were heavily armed, their horses deep-chested and long-legged. From the dust, they'd evidently ridden a long way, but the horses were breathing easily.

"Howdy," Jed said pleasantly as the men stopped beside them.

"Howdy."

Jonny's heart thumped in his throat as they looked shrewdly at Jed, at the well-filled wagon, and particularly at the boy on the wagon.

"We're on the trail of Coe and his outlaws," said one of the men. "We think they came this way."

"It's possible," answered Jed and waited for him to go on.

"We're from Pueblo," continued the man.

"Vigilantes?"

Jed asked the question cautiously, knowing he was on forbidden ground.

"That's right. Coe and his raiders rode into town and robbed three stores, killing the owners."

"Only you three after them?" asked Jed incredulously.

"We'll make out." The man was plainly impatient with the inference. "Is this the trail to the Roost?"

Jed nodded and the men galloped away. He looked after them and shook his head.

"Tenderfeet. Too bad. They was right nice-appearin' young men. Fool-hearted and hasty, but nice-appearin'. Probably hotheads that wouldn't listen to reason."

Goosebumps prickled Jonny's arms. The dust from their horses' hoofs hadn't settled yet, and Jed spoke like their time had already run out.

10

Cow Camp on the Vega

Jonny pulled up beside the chuck wagon, grinning triumphantly at Jed. He'd driven the wagon through the Canyon Road.

"Where's Charlie?" Jed asked a lean sunburned man who glanced up from his cooking as they drove up. "He ordered some provisions from Martin Hardy. This young sprout is Jonny Hardy, and I'm Jed Wilson."

"My name's Jim Holt. The boss was expecting you tomorrow, but if there's coffee on that pack horse, I'm sure glad you drove in tonight. Make yourself to home."

"Thanks, kindly," replied Jed, swinging from the saddle. "Where'd you say your boss is?"

"I didn't say," said Jim. "But he's gone to Trinidad."

"He didn't make mention of a trip to Trinidad. He told Martin he'd be here to receive this load. Say, what outfit is this?"

"The Goodnight," answered Jim, sniffing the stew and wrinkling his nose in disgust. "I've et rabbit stew so much my ears are pushing up my hat. Now what was I saying?"

"You ain't said nothing yet," retorted Jed. "What about Charlie?"

"He left in a hurry yesterday morning. A Mexican rode up all in a lather. Said Coe and his outlaws had taken over Trinidad. They were shootin' up the place. Free drinks for everyone and meals on the town. Seems their little game had been going on for ten or twelve hours. The Mexican wanted Goodnight to ride up and drive 'em out of town."

"Where was the marshal?" demanded Jed. "And the military?"

"Last the Mexican saw of the marshal, he was dancin' to the tune of bullets right in the street. He said Coe was boastin' he was settin' himself up as king of Trinidad."

"Sounds like someone's been drawin' a mighty long bow," said Jed doubtfully. "Sure it ain't a trick?"

"No, we ain't sure. Charlie didn't want to go, but this Mexican is a good friend of his. Owns a store in Trinidad and Coe's gang had wrecked it. Not only his, but they'd set out to wreck the town. Nobody was safe. They was all blind drunk, and you know how dead set Charlie is against drinkin'."

Everybody knew Mr. Goodnight's stand on whisky. He'd not tolerate swearing, gambling, or drinking in his camp. Any man who didn't follow those rules was paid off and told to get out.

"You sure got a grizzly by the tail if that Mexican wasn't telling the truth," said Jed. "How many men left in camp?"

"That just might be the grizzly," Jim answered grimly. "Charlie hired a new hand on the trail. That Indian raid cut down the outfit considerably. The man seemed honest enough. Said he'd had a lot of experience trailin' cattle. Charlie left him and Whitey Foster and me. Charlie studied about taking him, but decided if there was trouble in Trinidad he'd rather trust his own men.

"Me and Whitey wasn't too sold on the man. Don't know why, just somethin' about him. Whitey took part of the *remuda* down with the cows. Me and him were ridin' herd, and this hombre was supposed to try to sleep and still keep an ear open so nothin' would happen to the rest of the horses. When Whitey came in about midnight to change watch, the man was gone and so was the horses —about twenty-five head."

"Jed," exclaimed Jonny, "you reckon those was the horses that passed our camp?"

"Could be," said Jed. "Jim, you and Whitey's about rode out, ain't you? Looks like you could use a couple of greenhorns till Charlie gets back."

Jim's tired face brightened, then he looked doubtful.

"We sure could. We've been ridin' constant since

Charlie left, but we got no authority to hire anyone."

"Who said anything about hirin'?" roared Jed. "You're in trouble, ain't you? I've trailed cattle in my time, and the boy here knows how to ride. At least he could do as well as that." Jed pointed to the far side of the herd, where Whitey was asleep, slumped in his saddle, his chin on his chest.

"Fix Jonny and me a bite, and we'll take over for a while."

Jim grinned with pure pleasure when he found the sack of coffee.

"We've boiled our old grounds so much they're weaker'n a calf in a spring blizzard. Whitey says he's going to drink Cimarron water. Says it looks and tastes more like coffee than what we've been drinkin'."

Jonny and Jed saddled fresh horses and Jim dished up big plates of stew.

"Don't think I'll ever blame an Indian again for stealing horses so long as he eats 'em," said Jim. "I'm so hungry for a taste of something besides rabbit, the rattlesnakes scoot for cover when they see me comin'."

"Can't you kill a cow?" asked Jonny.

"The boss is runnin' so deep in the hole on account of that Indian raid, I ain't got the heart," explained Jim. "One cow every few days don't sound like much, but they'll tally up at the end of the road."

Jed nodded. He knew the hazards of trailing cows. Under the best circumstances it was risky business, but trailing through Comanche and Apache country, a man could never reckon his profit till the last day.

Jonny had no qualms against rabbit stew and stowed away two platefuls before he wiped his mouth on his sleeve and climbed into the saddle.

Whitey was coming slowly around the resting cattle, and they rode to meet him. Jed spoke softly. Whitey's head lopped loosely forward. Jed spoke again and Jonny backed away. Cowboys, awakened from a sound sleep, sometimes shot first and talked later. At the third call, Whitey came to with a start and glared at Jed.

"Where'd you come from?" he demanded.

"Fresh hands takin' over for a spell," explained Jed. Whitey looked at Jim, who was beckoning him in.

"Man, if you got past him, you got a job." Then Whitey saw Jonny. "This outfit must be going to the dogs if we have to turn it over to tadpoles."

Jonny flushed, but Jed laughed easily.

"We start 'em young in Robbers' Roost country," he drawled. "We feed 'em grizzly milk whilst they're bitsy babies and give 'em bullets to cut their teeth on. Soon as they git two teeth that hit we toss 'em a haunch of catamount meat. After that, they're on their own. Funny thing though, I ain't never seen one of them grizzly-fed babies go to sleep on the job."

Whitey, still dazed from sleep, grinned sheepishly.

"If you got any extry grizzly milk, I could do with a hefty swig. I started out to sing the cows to sleep.

Durned if my own music didn't turn tail and back-bite me."

"I'm really not a hand," explained Jonny. "Mr. Goodnight's a friend, and we're only helping out till you and Jim get some rest."

"Keep your horses saddled," warned Jed. "We ain't top hands and we might need help in a hurry."

They rode toward the herd. Whitey watched them turn, one to the left, the other to the right; then he went to the chuck wagon.

Jonny's horse knew what was expected. He held to a plodding walk. The saddle was a comfortable change from the hard wagon seat.

The wind that had blown all day died with the sunset. From the scrubby bushes a mockingbird whistled; meadow larks poised on the cholla and called to each other.

The shadow of Capulin Mountain crept over the chuck wagon, then farther and farther beyond, until it touched Jed and the sleeping herd. The clouds turned from pink to blue; then the light was gone.

The mountains loomed high, grown in that instant of twilight. They closed in the high prairies. There were only Jonny and Jed and the cattle. The stars hung above, shimmering blobs of light in the blackness.

Once a restless steer got to its feet. Jonny heard Jed call softly and the steer lay down again. When they met on the circle, Jed reined his horse.

"You makin' it all right, Jonny?"

"Uh-huh," he said, yawning fit to split his face. "Sing something," Jed said. "The cattle miss it."

"Can't you do it? I never sung to a cow in my life."

"My croakin' would start a stampede. There's another bull gettin' restless. Sing!" commanded Jed.

"What'll I sing? I don't know any cow songs."

"Whatever comes into your mind, but git started afore that critter takes it into his thick head to run."

Jonny searched frantically in his mind for a suitable song—a lullaby—any song. Then he began softly, drawing the tones out in a lonesome wail.

> "Old Dan Tucker was a fine old man,
> He washed his face in a frying pan.
> He combed his hair with a wagon wheel
> And died with the toothache in his heel."

He sang this three times before he could think of another. Then he sang "Buffalo Gal" and "Oh! Susannah."

The cattle hunched themselves down again, and the herd was quiet. Jonny sang church tunes and school tunes and a tune he'd learned sitting on the porch outside a dance hall. He sang till his throat was dry and the words ran together. After a while he didn't know what he was singing. This lasted until Jim came to relieve them.

"That forty winks put me right on top," Jim said. "Them tunes of yours are real fancy. You'll educate the cows out of our class, first thing you know."

Jonny wasn't interested in music-loving cows. He waited until Jed finished his lap, then they cantered back to the fire. Whitey lay with his mouth open. He hadn't bothered to unroll his blanket.

Jonny fumbled with the saddle buckles, too tired to see or reason how they fastened. Jed lifted the lid of the coffeepot and grunted with satisfaction.

He poured Jonny a cupful. There was no word of praise or thanks, and Jonny was halfway mad. He didn't expect a big to-do, but Jed might have noticed he'd done a man's work. Instead, all he got was a cup of black coffee.

"This sure is man's coffee," said Jed, smacking his lips. "Goes good after a long day."

"It sure does," agreed Jonny, choking and sputtering over the bitter stuff.

Jed tipped his cup and let the coffee gurgle down his throat. He poured himself another and hunkered down beside Jonny.

"Yes, sir, coffee like this evens up the day."

The old man's eyes were bloodshot, the lids raw from dust and weariness. His bones creaked as he eased himself into a more comfortable position. Nobody praised him for doing what had to be done. He was only thankful for a cup of strong coffee when it was all over.

Jonny looked at his own cup. If this was a man's reward, he'd accept it. He took a long swallow, then set the cup on the ground.

When he opened his eyes the sun was already up. Whitey was still sleeping. Others had taken over for Mr. Goodnight, and his men had returned. Jim was making breakfast.

"Didn't expect you to clean up Trinidad so soon," Jed was saying. "What happened?"

"Nothing," replied Mr. Goodnight. "The outlaws

heard we were coming. As we rode in one side of town they rode out the other. The shopkeepers boarded up their broken windows and unlocked the doors. The marshal got a new gun, and business went on as usual."

"Was that all?" cried Jonny.

He hadn't actually wanted bloodshed, but Mr. Goodnight deserved more glory than this. The men roared with laughter at his disappointment.

"They blasted a few shots," Chris Howe said, "but they weren't in top form."

"The vigilantes met and put up five hundred dollars for Coe, dead or alive." Jim Davis slapped his knee and laughed. "That town buzzed like a beehive. Everybody had something to do. There wasn't a man in town but his wife was lyin' at death's door, or his dozen kids were all down with measles, or his horse had fits. They had business in Denver or St. Joe or California. Not a man jack of 'em had any business in Robbers' Roost country."

"We met three men on the trail," Jonny remarked. "They said they were vigilantes from Pueblo."

"Poor devils," said John, softly.

From the silence, Jonny knew this was what they all thought. Poor devils. He wondered where they were now.

"Anything happen here?" asked Mr. Goodnight.

Jim told about the disappearance of the horses and the new hand. Jed added what he suspected.

"So that's the way the wind blew," said Mr. Goodnight disgustedly. "I suspected something of the kind."

"Maybe this was Coe's way of making trouble," suggested Jonny. "He threatened, you remember."

"Could be I played right into his hand." Jim handed Mr. Goodnight a plate of food which he took with a tired sigh. "Again, this rustler may be on his own and found a good chance to have the blame fall on someone else."

"Could be, but it ain't likely," Jed said sourly. "That's why they didn't make a stand against you in Trinidad. They'd done their dirty work."

Plainly the men all agreed with Jed. First the Indian raid, now the horses. Coe might not be able to run Mr. Goodnight out of the Black Mesa country, but he was doing all he could to make this trip a financial failure.

Jonny lay on his stomach and listened to Mr. Goodnight plan the search for the horses. As soon as they had eaten, two men were to go to pick up the trail of the horses Jed and Jonny had heard the night before. Others were sent to Willow Bar Crossing and Cold Springs, two probable places along the Cimarron Cutoff where wagon trains might be in need of stock. Everyone knew Coe's habit of turning his stolen stock into cash as soon as possible. Jed promised to keep an eye out around the Black Mesa. All but Jed and Jonny were to report back by sunup next morning.

11

The Black Mesa Trail

JED and Jonny started off in the cool of the morning. They left the team and pack horse with Mr. Goodnight, promising to return for them in two or three days. Jed held to the trail that led to the flat purple shadow outlined against the rising sun.

"The Black Mesa, Jonny," he said. "Robbers' Roost lays just off the tip. We'll be close enough soon to get a good view."

"Will we see the Cimarron Cutoff, Jed? I've always had a hankering to see that. It must be a sight."

" 'Tis when the Conestogas are comin' four abreast with their matched oxen. Most of the drivers are changin' to mules now. They're faster over the Cutoff. We won't go that far if we sight buffalo this side. That's Cheyenne and Arapaho country. They ain't as bad as the Apaches and Comanches, but still there's nothing gentle about them either. My own scalp ain't much, but I'd like to see yours get its full growth afore it's threatened."

"I'm kind of partial to a full head of hair, too," Jonny replied with a grin.

"Right around the Roost will be the best huntin'." Jed's faded blue eyes sparkled. "There's some mighty purty valleys around there with plenty of good water. When I was drivin' the Cutoff we could always depend on findin' buffalo and deer and antelope around there."

"You like this country, don't you, Jed."

"If I'd been a homesteadin' man, I'd have picked up a piece just this side of No-Man's-Land. In spring it's purty as a picture, with the green grass all scattered through with flowers. The Cimarron and Carrizo Creek draw lots of water—enough for a good-sized herd. Grass is good there, even in summer when pickings is scant on the hills."

"Now Coe's ruined it," Jonny said. "Nobody'd want to live there."

"Coe won't live forever."

Jed's voice carried such conviction that Jonny took his words for a promise. Might be Jed had a plan he wasn't babbling to the winds. He always kept a closed mouth about his comings and goings. Could be all this talk of taking Jonny to the Roost country had more to it than he let on.

Buffalo were scattered all over the high prairies. No need going clear to No-Man's-Land after them. There were plenty up on the Arkansas around Fort Lyon and Bent's Fort. Yes, Jed was a wily old codger. If he had other reasons for hunting near

Robbers' Roost, he could keep them to himself, and Jonny counted himself lucky to be a part of them.

At noon they stopped by a stream and rested the horses. Jed shot a prairie hen and Jonny built a fire under an overhanging cliff out of the wind. The hen was fat and tasty and hit the spot that had been nagging his middle for the last hour.

"What does the hideout look like, Jed?" he asked as he leaned against a boulder, his hat over his eyes to keep out the glare.

Jed chuckled, "I wondered when that question was comin' up. I can take you to a front-row seat if you're game."

"Sure I'm game. Where's the seat?"

"On top of the Black Mesa. I know an animal trail that leads up. From the rimrock you can practically look down the hideout's chimney."

"Honest?"

Jed squinted into the sun.

"We could get there by sundown. Yonder's the canyon trial. That takes us within a mile of the Roost."

"Suppose someone stops us?"

"If it's someone we know, we'll tell 'em the truth. I'm takin' you into buffalo and Injun country to give you a taste of excitement. They know Martin has kept you too close to home."

"Suppose we don't know them."

Jonny could hardly keep a quaver from his voice.

"Then I'm your grandpap takin' you back to your

ma's people in Arkansas. The trail leads right through
the Cherokee Strip and on to Fort Gibson. After all,
Coe don't own the road. He's just one of the hazards."

Jonny kicked dirt on the fire and ran to the creek
to scour the frying pan.

"Let's get going, Grandpap," he said as he fastened
the pan to the saddle.

Jed drank the rest of the coffee to keep from
wasting it. He left the grounds in the pot ready
for the next time.

"We'll save what's left of the hen," he said. "Might
be we won't want to build a fire tonight."

The going was faster when they struck the well-
traveled road. Jonny's heart throbbed in his throat
as he watched the Black Mesa loom larger and
larger against the sky. But he wasn't scared any
more, not the way he had been at home, just thinking about it. At home, the Black Mesa was a bogy-
word to frighten children with. Here it was a
mountain that shaved off the sky, sharp and flat, that
gathered storm clouds on its tableland and rolled
them down in streams to water the grasslands. The
long rolling uplands were broken by craggy sandstone hills and jagged rocks, strangely out of place
in the vast reaches of waving grass and flowers. Yet
they added a wild beauty, harsh and compelling.

Jed took a deep breath and lifted his face.

"Didn't I tell you she was purty, boy. A man
couldn't ask for more than a bit of this creation.
It's about as near heaven as an old sinner like me
will ever get."

He sat with his hat off, wind blowing his straggly hair. The air was thin and clear as spring water. Only the wind and the bird songs disturbed the immense stillness of the place.

"It ain't right a man should brand a place like this with his own deeds. Come on, boy. I'm going to show you how puny man is."

Coe won't live forever! Only this morning Jed had said those words. Jonny turned cold. A sudden fear twisted his insides.

"Jed, what are you going to do? You ain't going to shoot Coe, are you?"

Jed whirled on him.

"What's eatin' you, Jonny?" he roared. "You puttin' me in the same class with that lowdown outlaw. Why I ought to jerk you off that horse and tan your britches."

Jonny laughed hysterically. "You had me scared for a minute. This place and the Mesa and . . . and . . . I was just scared, that's all."

"The law will get Coe," promised Jed. "He put his head in the noose when he stole those horses from the fort. The law will get him, and he'll have a fair trial. The law will give him that. But he'll come to his end like all horse thieves." And he began to whistle "Hanging From a Sour Apple Tree."

"They'll have to hunt a long time to find a sour apple tree in this country," said Jonny, laughing.

"There's plenty of cottonwoods," replied Jed, unconcerned.

Another hour of traveling brought them close to

the hideout. They followed the hills that rimmed Carrizo Creek, keeping close to the rocky uplifts where the shadows were already purple. They crossed the creek a mile below the Roost. Jed let the horses drink while Jonny filled the canteens with fresh water. They twisted between the hills for another mile down to the edge of the Mesa.

"The trail up the Mesa should be just beyond that big red rock." Jed pointed to a wind-carved knob of glittering sandstone. "That one that juts out from the mountain like a buffalo hump."

Jonny studied the Mesa wall. It rose in a series of terraces of jumbled rocks. If Jed said the trail was there, it would be there, but the horses would have to be part mountain goat to climb it.

They rounded the humped rock and entered a short canyon. The floor was hard packed, showing a clearly marked path which angled steeply upward until it reached the first terrace. The trail widened, permitting surer footing as it twisted around boulders and skirted deep cuts, but continued its steady rise. Here the sun was hidden, although the peaks around them were still bright. Blotches of purple shadows crossed the trail.

Jonny felt alone, shut off from his kind, even though his horse traveled close on the heels of Jed's. There was only the *thud, thud,* of hoofs, hardly louder than the thudding of his heart.

Suddenly, from somewhere above them, a shower of pebbles and small stones hurtled down the path.

Jed pointed to a great stone just ahead. They circled it quickly and crowded close in its deep shadow. They waited and Jed drew his gun from the holster. He shook his head when Jonny readied his own rifle.

The clomping feet came nearer. Whoever was coming was not yet aware there were others on the trail. The hoofbeats came steadily on, heavily, carelessly. Then a dark shape ambled into view. Jed chuckled softly.

"A mule deer. Goin' down for water."

The deer had not winded them and he plodded on, his great ears flapping with every step. Jonny began to breathe again.

"That means there's likely no one on the trail but us," Jed reasoned. "We'll push the horses."

The trail now followed a terrace of black rock half hidden by a scattering of piñon and cactus. A flock of towhees that had settled for the night darted up in fright. A bobcat leaped across the path, and the horses snorted in fear. A bullbat soared above them, its booming cry deepening the vast loneliness. The unending reaches of space crowded in on Jonny, pushed him down, shriveled him, until he was only a speck crawling up the mountainside. This was what Jed meant when he called man a puny creature. No man could live forever; but this Mesa, these towering spiked rocks, the wild plains, would live on and on.

At long last the horses, heaving and blowing, stumbled onto the worn cap rock.

"We'll unsaddle and turn 'em loose," said Jed. "They've earned a rest."

Jed's matter-of-fact words broke the black spell that held Jonny. He jumped down and unfastened the buckles. The horses began to graze on the clump grass that somehow had managed to send down roots between the rocks.

"Now we'll take a peek at the hideout while there's light. We may want to leave before sunup," said Jed with a sly grin.

Jed made his way toward the point of the Mesa, keeping well behind the outcropping stones. Jonny crept along behind him, stepping lightly although he was high above the prairie floor.

12

Robbers' Roost

JONNY crouched beside Jed and clung to the rocks.
Below lay a narrow green valley, cut through
by the silver water of Carrizo Creek. It lay hushed
and undisturbed, shut in by a cluster of shimmering
hills on the one side and the Black Mesa on the
other. Jed pointed to a hill, whipped raw by the
winds.

"Robbers' Roost," he whispered.

In the sunset it looked no different from the other
desolate crags. But the talk was that its flat top
bristled with guns.

"There's the hideout just below us."

The house perched on a windy knoll in the curve
of the creek where it cut sharply around the foot of
the Mesa. It was built from the red rocks of the
Roost and blended so perfectly into the mountain
that from a distance it could easily be mistaken for
a heap of stones. There were no windows—only a
row of black dots, shoulder high.

"Them little dots are gun sights," Jed explained. "They ain't more'n four or five inches across on the outside, but I heered tell they flange out eighteen or twenty inches on the inside. That way a man can maneuver a gun and make a clean sweep of the valley."

"Where's the door?" asked Jonny.

"Facin' the Roost," replied Jed. "If things get too hot in the hideout, they can make for the mountain. Once up there they've got everything purty much their own way."

"Yeah. Two men with Sharps rifles could do it. How do they get up?"

"Don't know. They've kept a close mouth about that. These hills are full of caves. Maybe there's a secret passage."

"Wonder where everyone is?" asked Jonny. "It's so still it gives me the creeps."

"Don't know," answered Jed. "But I ain't really wantin' to find out. Think you'd be interested in some of that prairie hen now?"

Jed was already on the way back to their gear. Keeping his eyes on the hideout, Jonny twisted and turned until he found a comfortable seat among the rocks.

The place looked deserted. There was no sound or movement, no specks of light from the portholes. Gradually the valley became dark. The stars were beginning to show.

The wind, which had blown all day, died down.

In a gnarled tree on the slope of the Mesa, birds
rustled and twittered. The night sounds carried a
long way in the thin air—frogs booming along the
creek, crickets creaking in the bunch grass, mocking-
birds trying to outsing each other.

Jed felt his way through the darkness and handed
Jonny a cold drumstick. It tasted good. He hadn't
known he was hungry.

"Moon's coming up," he said, waving the drumstick toward a light in the east.

Jed looked up. The pale glow wavered, then
swirled up wild and red against the sky.

" 'Tain't the moon," said Jed grimly. "That's fire."

"Indian camp?"

"Too big."

"Prairie fire?"

"It don't spread like a prairie fire."

This fire didn't spread. It licked high in the sky,
tipping the mountains and buttes with rosy pink.

"It's close to Willow Bar Crossing," Jed said.
"That's a raid on a wagon train. Cheyennes or Comanches, probably."

Jonny's knees began to tremble. His teeth chat-
tered, and the trembling spread through his body
until he couldn't stand.

He had come over the Santa Fe Trail, but he'd
been a baby then and couldn't remember. All his
life he'd heard tales of Indian attacks on the wagon
trains. Ma and Pa had told him how they had hidden
behind rocks, behind wagons, in the tall grass, any-

where that gave them a chance against the fury of the raiders. The bullwhackers and drovers had told him. Jed had told him. A hundred times Jed had told him. He'd listened and asked for more. But all their talk had been only tales.

Now he saw the red flames. It was as if they scorched his skin. The crying children, the screaming animals, the din of guns—it was all true. They were there in those twisting tongues of fire. This was real.

It was real to Jed, too, hunched behind him, his breath ripping through his throat. Jed's body pressed against Jonny, crushing him against the rock of the Black Mesa, shielding him, hiding him.

A wave of terror swept over him. Had the old man gone crazy? Had the crimson blaze snapped his reason?

"Jed! Jed!" Jonny kicked and struggled to free himself. "Jed, it ain't here. It's a long way off."

Jed dropped his gun and laughed weakly.

"Guess this ain't my fight, son," he said, half ashamed. "But when you've fit as many fights as I have with those bloody Injuns, your body don't seem to wait for your mind to catch up. You jump and think afterward. Did I hurt you, boy?"

"Gosh, no." Jonny laughed in relief. "You only scared the living daylights out of me. You had me thinking I was about to be scalped."

"A man's scalp sits mighty loose in this country," Jed answered gravely.

Fumbling through his vest pockets for a twist of tobacco, he watched the distant light. It had faded now, leaving only a faint glow. This, too, died away.

The hideout below was still silent and dark. Nothing had changed in the valley.

"Here's your blanket," Jed said. "Shake it before you wrap up. You might find yourself sleeping with pack rats or chipmunks or somethin'."

Jonny was suddenly cold. He wrapped the blanket around him and propped himself against a boulder. The moon was rising. Cholla and juniper took dusky shapes along the Mesa slope. Wisps of white mist rose from Carrizo Creek, twisting, writhing, then vanishing in the wind.

The blackness of Robbers' Roost hung so close Jonny shut his eyes. He wondered what Ma was doing now. Probably setting the bread to rise on the back of the stove. Matt most likely was sleeping with his wooden gun.

He didn't know how long he slept, but the grip of Jed's fingers woke him. The valley was in an uproar. Coe and his outlaws were back.

The moon was high. The hideout, the creek, animals and men, were boldly magnified in the white light. The valley thundered with a surging mass of terrified horses and cattle and savage men. The wind carried the clamor and din to the Mesa top. Jonny and Jed could hear the curses and shouts as plainly as if they were a part of it. The outlaws made no effort to cover their trail with silence.

Coe was everywhere, lashing out with his whip, now in the middle, now veering aside to block the escape of some hapless animal. He cursed and slashed, and the hills echoed the screams and bellows of pain.

Jonny had never seen this Coe. The Coe he knew was cruel and ruthless enough, but this man was inhuman, fiendish in his brutality, and his men were cut from the same hide. There were Indians among them, and they were no more savage than the white men.

Sickened by the sight, Jonny hid his face. No wonder Pa and the men in town held their peace. They knew this Coe.

At last the animals were penned and the men gathered in front of the hideout. Coe began to talk. Then Jonny learned the animals had come from the wagon train. The outlaws of Robbers' Roost had fired the wagons.

"Them's Cheyennes down there," whispered Jed, fearful his voice might carry. "I savvy their talk."

"You mean Coe would join a Cheyenne raiding party?"

Jed squeezed his arm.

"Listen. There's some ruckus amongst them."

Jed inched along the cap rock, keeping well out of sight. A moving shadow, a loosened stone slipping down the Mesa, and their hides wouldn't make good sieves.

A quarrel was brewing between the Cheyennes

and the outlaws. The talk was in Cheyenne, and Jonny couldn't follow it.

"What they fighting about, Jed?"

"Over the loot. The Cheyennes think they're not gettin' their fair share."

Coe gave an order and the men drove a dozen horses from the corral and turned them over to the Indians. Still they argued. Coe swore and threatened. The Indians waved their guns and yelled. The excited horses reared and were subdued by a bloody lash.

"They stole some whisky," explained Jed. "The Injuns want part of it. Coe told them to go back to the wagons and get their share."

Jonny's thumping heart almost choked him. A gun fight between the two factions might end everyone's troubles.

But the dispute ended without bloodshed. Coe handed over a hogshead which evidently contained whisky. The Indians seized it and raced away to the north, driving their newly acquired horses before them.

"Looks like Coe met his match in that big Injun." Jed shook with silent laughter. "Now I reckon they'll likker up on what they held out."

Instead, Coe began to issue orders. "Dick, you and Jackson stay here out of sight. Tomorrow pick up the Goodnight horses on the other side of the Roost."

Jed touched Jonny's knee to make sure he was listening.

"Put 'em with this new stock and drive 'em back to the trail," Coe went on. "Hold 'em at Cold Springs until the train catches up, or what's left of it. They'll be beggin' for horses, and they'll pay whatever you ask."

"Suppose they recognize their own stock, Captain?"

"They ain't in any position to argue. The rest of us will ride to Pueblo. A stage is leaving Raton to-morrow for the States. There's a shipment of gold from Elizabethtown on it. After you get rid of the stuff, head for Denver. We'll meet you there."

Coe and his riders disappeared between the hills. Dick and Jackson turned their horses loose to graze. Light gleamed faintly through the portholes. After a time this disappeared. Robbers' Roost was quiet once more.

"You've seen 'em, Jonny." Jed's shoulders drooped as he picked up his blanket. "That's the way they work. Strike. Kill. Burn. Then before the moon is down, they're off to start again."

"Jed, let's find those horses and take 'em back."

Jed whirled and stared in amazement. "Boy, have you lost your senses? You seen what went on here tonight. Ain't that enough?"

"They're Mr. Goodnight's horses, not Coe's," said Jonny. "We know where they are. Back of that mountain." He pointed to the Roost. "I saw what happened, and I heard what they said. But we've got to get them."

"I don't cotton to stirring up a rattler's nest," replied Jed, starting toward their horses. "Especially with you along."

"You mean you'd try it if you was alone?"

"I didn't say that," said Jed, gruffly. "Don't go to puttin' words in my mouth. What we'd best do is ride to the Vega and report. Then if the outfit wants to make a showdown, it's their funeral."

"We haven't time," persisted Jonny. "You heard Coe say to sell them tomorrow."

"Why are you so all fired up to save Goodnight's horses?" demanded Jed.

"It's because of Charlie, my longhorn," Jonny said fiercely. "Coe killed Red Leaf, and I had to pay for it with Charlie. If I can take those horses from him, I'll think I've paid him back—halfway, anyhow."

Jed was silent a long time, thinking it over, weighing the chances. Too long for the boy.

"If you don't come, I'll go by myself," he said finally. "I'll slip away in the dark and go."

There was that in his voice which reminded Jed of Martin Hardy, a stubborn, stony persistence once his course was set. The moonlight seemed to chisel away the boyish roundness of the face, leaving the sharp line of the jaw and the firm set of the mouth, so like Martin's. It made him look taller too.

"You mean it, boy? You'd slip away in the dark?"

"It's for Charlie," Jonny said simply. "I'd hate to go alone, but if you won't come, I will. Seems it's something I've got to do."

Without another word of protest Jed caught up the horses.

"When we get to the bottom we'll scout around and see how the land lays," he said as he started his horse over the cap rock and down the Mesa trail.

13

A Bold Plan

"KEEP in the shadows," Jed said when they were safely at the bottom of the Mesa. "We'd show like two black cats in the snow out there in the moonlight."

They pulled up beside a rock which thrust up a full twenty feet from the earth. The moon was still almost an hour high.

"Got a plan?" asked Jed.

Jonny thought the matter over. Jed was respecting the manful assertion he'd made back on the Mesa top. He must weigh every step and show Jed it wasn't childish anger that had set him against Coe. It wasn't only Charlie. It was Ma, crying in her apron, and the helpless droop of Pa's shoulders. It was the love Matt had for his wooden gun, and the look in Sam's eyes as he carried the hot irons to Coe. But these things he couldn't speak of, not even to Jed.

"Well," he began cautiously, "what do you think

of trying to locate the horses while the moon's up.
Then we can tell whether to swing 'em out or
wait. We could cross the Carrizo here, but it's risky.
The horses in the corral would be dead certain to
make a ruckus."

"That's my idea, too," Jed agreed.

"What say we head south down the creek a ways
and come back up behind that rim of hills?"

Jed nodded and they started off, keeping well
away from the bank. Anyone with an eye to the
portholes in the house at Robbers' Roost had a
sweeping view as far as the bend in the stream. As
long as Jonny and Jed kept the point of the Mesa
between them and the hideout they were reason-
ably safe. Still they kept to the shadows.

They traveled half a mile or more before they
felt sufficiently hidden to attempt a crossing. The
water was low and they walked the horses some
distance down the creek bed. The rim of rocks on
the opposite bank formed a palisade with occasional
breaks which permitted access to the grasslands beyond. They entered one of these gaps and turned
back north, hugging the rocks. A mockingbird was
singing close by. Somewhere far off a cow bawled,
probably one in the corral. Robbers' Roost rose before them in all its harshness.

Jonny searched for the hideout but couldn't dis-
tinguish it among the low buttes and rock abut-
ments. They went slowly, fearful of the consequences
if a metal shoe should strike a stone noisily. As

they neared the mountain the restless milling of the penned stock deadened the soft padding of their own horses' hoofs.

The wall of the mountain formed one side of the corral. Thus, a guard from the top of the Roost had a sweeping view of the corral, the hideout, and all the approaches within three hundred yards.

"Reckon there's a guard up there?" Jonny asked, eyeing the forbidding crags.

"Could be," replied Jed. He searched the rocks for movement or the dull glow of a gun barrel. "I'd rather take a beatin' than cross that strip of light."

The portholes in the hideout were still dark, but the jagged shadows might well hide others than themselves.

"Jonny," he whispered at last, "can you ride like the Injuns when they sight buffalo?"

"You mean holding to the pommel and hanging down on the far side of the horse? I ain't good at it," he said doubtfully.

"It's an old trick that wouldn't fool an open-eyed baby," went on Jed. "But we got to count on that guard up there, if there is one, bein' half asleep."

"I'll try." Jonny slipped out of the saddle. Keeping one foot in the stirrup and clinging to the saddle horn, he swung himself alongside his horse.

"That's right," said Jed. "Now let the horse kind of meander like he was croppin' grass." He struck the pony lightly. "I'll meet you yonder in the shadows."

Without guiding hands on the reins, the pony lowered his head and began to graze. He moved slowly, lipping up the buffalo grass, sauntering away from the Roost, going farther and farther into the white meadow.

"Git back, you blasted dumbhead," Jonny cried.

He tried to edge the horse around with his shoulder. He rammed it with his head, he pleaded and coaxed, but the animal only continued its wayward wandering.

Jonny was tired. His fingers, gripped about the pommel, began to cramp. The cramps spread to his arms, his shoulders. He couldn't hold on much longer. Then he kicked the horse in the flank. It whirled, exposing him to the full view of the Roost. Desperately, he worked the fingers of his right hand along the reins until he felt them tighten in his grasp.

"Now, git."

The horse turned and galloped toward the Roost. Jonny's head snapped with every beat of the flying hoofs. He felt his fingers slipping; then Jed's firm hands caught him.

"I—I just about didn't make it," Jonny said shakily.

"You done all right," Jed answered. "Say, I been hearin' horses. The echoes are so bad in these hills I can't make out where the sound's comin' from. Could be them in the corral."

"Let's go on," Jonny suggested. "Coe said they was here."

A hundred yards farther along the cliff they rounded

a spur of rock. This was the end of the mountain, but the adjacent butte stretched out like an encircling arm. Enclosed within the walls was a bit of meadowland. The entrance was a high narrow gap, less than twenty feet in width. Jed's horse whinnied. From within the meadow came an answer. Jed and Jonny flung themselves forward, grasped the noses of the horses, and waited.

A fox slipped past them in the light. From somewhere behind him, Jonny heard the quick frantic squeal of a small animal.

"They're in there, Jonny," Jed whispered at long last. "I'll drive 'em out."

"I'll go."

Jonny's tongue was stiff and dry. He could hardly form the words.

"You'll do nothin' of the kind," snapped Jed. "You'll stay right here. Let 'em wander out in the light, but don't show yourself." He laid his hand on Jonny's knee. "If you hear shootin', boy, don't wait for nothin'. Head south for the Cimarron. Keep goin' till you reach the Vega. Understand?"

"Sure."

Jed disappeared through the gap. The pony, sensing the boy's tenseness, stamped nervously. The minutes passed. The moon hung above the prairie like a golden pumpkin, sinking lower and lower. The graying light veiled the juniper and the cholla. Still Jed did not return. There was only that muffled treading within the gap.

A wolf howled. Another answered. From far among
the hills came a chorus of long wailing cries. A
lean form slunk from the rocks close by and loped
across the plains. Jonny's scalp rose. The lobos were
gathering for the hunt. The pony trembled and
cold sweat rolled down Jonny's face. He gripped his
rifle.

It was then he saw the man at the far end of
the gap. He was standing close against the cliff, as
if he were waiting for Jed. He must have been on
guard in the meadow, for he wasn't yet aware of
Jonny.

Jonny raised his rifle. The man didn't move.
He seemed to be facing toward Jed, who was somewhere among the horses. Jonny's hands shook so
he couldn't hold the rifle still. Suppose he missed
and the sound of the shot brought the outlaws

upon them. He lowered the gun. Better use the knife. There'd be no noise then.

He slipped from the horse. The knife was cold in his clammy hands. He felt his way, silent as a cat. Strike quick! Strike, then slink into the shadows. Now was the time. Now. Desperate and nearly blinded by hot tears, he hit out with the knife. It clattered against hard stone.

Jonny broke into wild sobbing. It wasn't a man. It was only a pillar of stone, carved by the wind. He hadn't killed a man. He hadn't had to kill, after all. He ran to his horse, wiping away tears he hadn't realized were falling on his sleeve.

The first of the horses plodded through the gap. Jed was moving them slowly. On they came, and Jonny lost count. The moon was down, the stars pale points of light. At last he felt Jed's light touch on his arm, and they fell in behind the Goodnight horses, pointing them toward the Vega.

14

"Drop the Guns!"

JONNY twisted about in the saddle. Behind him the thin gold rim of the sun was rising through the haze of dust. Lavender shadows filled the dips in the slow-rising hills.

For the last three hours Jed had held the horses to an easy lope—not hurrying them, not letting them lag. But the miles between them and the Roost stretched out. Now the horses were beginning to stumble and falter.

Jonny was tired too. His muscles hurt clean to the tips of his ears. His insides griped and bellowed like a drought-starved steer. He tried to remember if he'd eaten the drumstick last night on the Mesa. Just knowing he had, might ease the gnawing. He wasn't sure but what he'd dropped it when the fire blazed up. He drew in his belt to the last notch. If he got any hungrier, it wouldn't hold up his pants.

"Jed, what do boots taste like?" he asked with a wry grin.

"Kind of sorry eatin', so I've heered." Jed looked at him searchingly. Then he raised in his stirrups and studied the trail behind them.

"I'm about to find out," Jonny muttered.

"Tell you what," Jed said. "The horses need rest. There's an arroyo over the brow of that far hill. This time of year the sinks are full of water. Real good grass, too."

"For us?" Jonny asked plaintively.

"Ninny, you ain't that far gone. You can last four . . . five more miles."

"There's sure to be snakes or pack rats there." Jonny grinned mischievously and smacked his lips.

"Shut up," said Jed. "Once on the Jornada we was down to eatin' rattlesnakes. But let me tell you, I got to be a lot hungrier than I am now before I stoop so low."

The arroyo was all that Jed said it was. Lush grass for the horses, water, and thickets of sand plums, wild grapes, and a few stunted trees.

"Good cover for turkeys," remarked Jonny.

"Just what I was thinkin'," answered Jed. "I'll hold the horses, and you see what you can scare up."

Turkey hunting wasn't new to Jonny. He'd kept Ma supplied all winter. In a place like this he'd be certain to flush several. He looked around the trees, expecting to see them scratching among the dried needles, but they weren't there. A covey of scaled quail rose up, but he let them pass. He could only hope to bring down one, and that would be much too small for a hunger as great as his.

Suddenly, he saw a glint of brown through the thicket. The turkeys were feeding on the other side, so it was a chancy shot, but no matter. As long as he could see that bit of brown he'd get his bird.

He pulled the trigger. There was a roar of pain, and out of the thicket rose the biggest, maddest bear he'd ever seen. All its white teeth showing against a red throat, it charged toward Jonny in injured fury.

The horse reared. Jed yelled. The bear came on. Jonny rammed in another bullet. The bear was close. It was bigger than a mule deer. Bigger than a buffalo. Jonny pulled the trigger, and the bear toppled. Jed came tearing down the hill, shouting like a Comanche.

"I shot a bear, Jed." Jonny whooped and hollered and pointed to the beast on the ground. "Did you see me? It's a bear. Looky. A bear!"

"You sure did," said Jed admiringly. "A right nice little bear. Just the right size for eatin'."

"Little!" roared Jonny. "It's the biggest bear I ever saw. It was coming like a cyclone."

He stared at the bear. It was a young two-year-old, hardly as big as Matt. It looked kind of pitiful lying there with its paw over its nose. Jonny glanced at Jed and grinned.

"Funny how fast that bear growed as he came

out of the bushes. I swear, Jed, an eight-foot puma won't ever look as big to me as that bear did."

"Yeah," Jed answered seriously. "I've had 'em grow on me like that. But he was a spunky little codger, I'll say that for him. Good thing you got him. Given a few years, he'd been a killer."

Jed skinned the bear, stripping the hide off neatly. He cut off the hindquarters and threw the rest to one side for the wolves and the coyotes. Immediately, out of nowhere came a flock of magpies, falling to it with harsh chattering.

Jonny built a fire and put on the coffeepot while Jed slapped some bear steaks into the pan.

Later, when Jonny couldn't eat another mouthful, he leaned against a great boulder and patted his stomach.

"Feel better?" asked Jed.

"Stuffed so tight my eyes won't shut," he answered.

Jed sat down beside him and stretched his legs.

"Jed," said Jonny, "if you'd been Dick or Jackson, what would you've done this morning when you found the horses gone?"

"Right off I can't say, not bein' an outlaw. What you drivin' at?"

"Would you have hunted the Goodnight horses or taken the rest of the stock to Cold Springs like Coe said?"

"Let's see," said Jed. "If I took time to hunt the horses, I might lose out on sellin' at Cold Springs. If I went to the Springs and got only half what

Coe expected . . . ding blast it, boy, Coe's got me between a rifle and a pistol either way I move. What would you do?"

"I'd go on to Cold Springs. Course I'd give a quick look around first, but I wouldn't dare show up in Denver, like he said, with no money at all. I'd be a dead duck, sure."

"Then you think a bird in the hand's worth two in the bush."

"Yeah," said Jonny. "I'd take a chance on knocking down a little extra money somewhere along the way."

"You don't think they're on our trail, then?" Jed asked contemplatively.

"I wouldn't be if I was them," reasoned Jonny. "On account of I wouldn't know when the horses disappeared. Whoever took 'em could have had an eight- or ten-hour start. We could have if we'd only knowed."

"You're a keen one," Jed said, chuckling quietly. "In that case, we don't need to worry. We're safe as——"

A shot blasted the morning stillness as a bullet struck the boulder against which they were leaning. Another scattered the fire, sending up a shower of sparks.

"Drop your guns and come out with your hands up."

"We've got you, you low-down rustlers."

Stiff with fear, Jonny got to his feet. Jed swore

at his own carelessness. The men had slipped up behind them as they rested.

"Well, shoot me for a coyote if it ain't the old man and the kid," said one.

"What you hidin' behind that rock for, you old half-wit?" demanded the other. "It's a wonder we didn't kill you."

They turned and looked into the astonished faces of Whitey Foster and Jim Holt from the Goodnight camp.

"A blind man knows his own friends," roared Jed. "Next time you two whippersnappers mistake me for a rustler, I'll pistol-whip you, so help me I will. I've a dodgasted notion to do it right now."

Jim and Whitey laughed. They knew Jed was only blowing off steam for being caught napping.

"We're real sorry," apologized Whitey. "But when we seen the Goodnight horses and no one in sight, we figured you was hid out, ready to take a pot shot at us."

"It's really the breakfast we're holdin' you up for," said Jim, eyeing the leftover steaks. "You can put your hands down now if you give us some."

Jed turned to the fire, madder than a wet cat. He fumed and sputtered as he made fresh coffee.

"Where'd you pick up the horses?" Whitey asked curiously.

"Where you yeller-bellied, lily-fingered cow drivers are too scared to show your faces. At the Roost.

Now keep your traps shut before I mistake your windpipes for bear meat."

Jim and Whitey gaped in amazement. Jed didn't see fit to tell any more, so Jonny didn't volunteer anything. Now that his knees had stopped quaking he felt the same way Jed did. Last night he thought he'd never forget those savage outlaws. Now, the first time his stomach was full and there was a nice warm rock to rest against, he'd got to talking big. How did he know how an outlaw reasoned? Could have been Dick and Jackson as easy as Jim and Whitey. It was mighty funny how brave—or careless—a fellow could get when the sun was up.

While the men ate, Jonny cleaned up camp and Jed saddled their horses.

"You might take Mr. Goodnight a haunch of bear," Jed said as he rolled up the meat in the hide and fastened it to Jonny's saddle. "Might be a change from all that jack rabbit Jim's been handin' out."

Jim grinned in relief. Jed was over his temper, and they were all forgiven.

By late afternoon they came upon the Goodnight cattle. As the horses trotted over the rise the camp burst into excitement.

"Jed and Jonny took 'em from the Roost," Jim said. "Right from under Coe's nose."

"Jed, you sly old coyote," exclaimed Mr. Goodnight. "How did you find them?"

"Coe told us where they was."

"I'll give you the horses if I swallow that," Mr. Goodnight hooted.

"He didn't aim to." Jed grinned and rolled his tobacco to the other cheek. "We happened to be hanging over the cap rock on the Black Mesa admirin' the view. Mighty purty view from up there. It'd do your soul good to see it."

The cowboys laughed. Trust Jed to make the tale good.

"It might, but what about my hide?" laughed Mr. Goodnight.

The drovers crowded around, laughing and joking. Whitey turned the herd over to the wrangler, who took charge of Jed's and Jonny's horses too. Jonny was embarrassed at the unexpected attention while Jed limped stiffly to the fire and the coffeepot.

"Hmmm," he sighed. "There ain't nothing like cow-camp coffee. It puts the legs right back under a man."

The men waited, their eyes glistening. Jed hunkered down within easy reach of the pot.

"I wouldn't have done it if it hadn't been for the boy, here," he began. "He had an old score to settle with Coe. You know about his calf." The men nodded. They'd heard the story. "I tried to talk him out of it. I'd have strapped him right there on the Mesa if it would've done any good. As for me, I'd have left the horses right there and you could whistle for 'em," he said seriously. "But for the boy, it was somethin' he owed to the longhorn. Least I could do was to go along and help."

Jonny flushed to the roots of his hair. The men hung on Jed's words. He told the story as it happened, but it lost nothing in the telling. Jonny looked into the glowing coals of the cook fire, and he could see again the dreadful scene which took place at the foot of the Black Mesa. Jed even told how Jonny had tried to kill the man on guard. He had confided the story to Jed as they left the Roost, and they had laughed over it.

"It was the Lord's blessing it turned out to be nothin' but a rock," Jed said. "But it would have been all the same if it had been an outlaw. I'm proud the boy's my friend."

The tale ended with Jed bringing out the hindquarters of the bear.

"Here's what's left of the toughest little scrapper this side of the Spanish Peaks. Jonny brought him down with two shots. I doubt I could've done better."

He held up the hide. It was right sizable the way he stretched it out. The men fingered it, pointing out battle scars, and guessing what the skin was worth. Jonny was so proud his shirt was hard put to cover his chest.

"I always miss the excitement," complained one of the cowboys.

"We had our share," replied Mr. Goodnight.

"What happened?" asked Jed.

"You remember the three vigilantes you met on the trail? We found them. Every one with a bullet in his back."

Jonny rolled over and hid his face. How had he and Jed managed to escape?

15

"Stand Up and Be Counted!"

Jonny started off the next morning in a rosy cloud of happiness. Mr. Goodnight had given him his own knife sheath to make up for the buffalo he hadn't shot. The sheath was old and dirty, but Jonny thought it was beautiful as he watched it swing smartly with the lurching of the wagon. With the horses rested and nothing in the wagon except the bear hide, they made good time.

Not far from Black Wolf's camp they passed a platoon of soldiers. They nodded but did not stop to talk. Jed turned and watched them canter down the road. Then they began to see others along the trails leading into the hills.

"Hmmmm," said Jed, spattering the dust with a stream of tobacco juice. "Wonder what's up. Coe must've stirred up a hornet's nest to get all them fancy-pantses in the saddle."

Jonny grinned. Jed's opinion of the cavalry was well known. But even as he smiled, a nagging apprehension of danger swept over him. He wanted to get home. Word may have already reached Coe of the missing Goodnight horses.

"Did anyone in town know we was going to the Vega?" he asked.

"Just about everybody," replied Jed. "Your pa wanted word spread around. He figured he'd paid for your protection."

For protection, yes. But not for interference in the outlaw's plans. For the first time Jonny began to see the enormity of his act and to realize its far-reaching effects. There'd be no peace in the Cimarron Valley if Coe ever suspected he and Jed had taken the horses. What would Pa say? Could he wait for the law now? And Ma? Jonny struck the horses and sent them galloping down the road.

When he reached the ranch at sundown he saw a fire blazing under the cottonwood tree. Beside it lolled half a dozen soldiers.

"Hi, Jonathan," one of them called.

It was his old acquaintance, the sergeant.

"What's up?" asked Jonny, jumping from the wagon.

"Orders from headquarters," answered the sergeant. "This time we're to get Coe, dead or alive. That branding party he put on with Government horses opened some big eyes. Then last night he robbed the stage out of Raton. There's nobody left to tell how it happened."

Jonny didn't need to be told. Not after what he had seen in the moonlight from the Black Mesa.

Enflamed by the attack on the wagons and angered by his own weakness with the Indians, Coe would be a madman.

"What are you doing here?"

The soldiers glanced swiftly at each other, then looked into the fire. Some of them knew Jonny. All had seen him around the post. The sergeant hesitated, choosing his words carefully.

"We know Coe comes here for shelter. Every fort in this part of the country has been alerted. We're going to make it so hot he'll have to hunt cover. We want to be here when he comes."

So that was it. They figured the Hardy ranch was the place he'd run to. They hadn't forgotten about that horse with the Government brand, after all. Jonny picked up the reins and started for the barn.

"Jonny," Jed said, looking around to see that they were alone. "If I was you, I'd not mention anything about the Goodnight horses."

"What do you take me for, a blabber mouth?" growled Jonny, weak with fear.

"I know, I know," Jed answered hastily. "Just wanted to make sure. Your pa's got to know—and maybe your ma. With Coe hounded out of every hidin' hole, he's apt to show his true color, that is if he should come."

Jonny shook his head impatiently. Coe wouldn't come, with soldiers hunkered down on their doorstep.

"You suppose we're the only ones they're watching?"

"Wouldn't think so," replied Jed. "Judgin' from all we saw, there's soldiers thick as magpies hangin' around every ranch in the valley."

The thought didn't ease Jonny's mind. In that case, Coe would be desperate. With every door closed to him and soldiers beating the trails, he'd be hard put to find a hole to crawl into.

"Here, take this." Jed handed him the bear hide. "It'll be good for a lot of talk. Try to stall around till your pa gets home. I'll go on to the post and report."

Jonny opened the door. Ma's smile never had looked so good. Matt tore across the room and hurled himself into his brother's arms.

"Jonny! Jonny! Ma, Jonny's home! Hey, what's this?" He seized the bear hide, and the remains of the hindquarters slid across the floor. "Looky. Looky. Jonny brought me a bear skin."

He draped the smelly hide over his head and growled, but Jennie snatched it away.

"You was all washed for supper," she scolded. "Now look at you."

"Aw, let him look at it," Jonny said tolerantly. "A little bear smell won't hurt him."

"Did Jed shoot it?" asked Ma, rescuing the hindquarters from under the table.

"Naw. I did." Jonny tried to speak with all the

boredom and indifference he could muster. As if bear shooting was an every-morning occurrence, like milking or feeding the horses.

"Of course, Jonny killed it," shouted Matt. "He went hunting, didn't he? Jonny always gets what he goes after."

And sometimes he gets more than he bargained for, Jonny thought grimly, as he reached for the milk pail.

"I'll do the chores and tell you about it later."

Matt tagged after him, wrapped to the chin in the bear hide.

"You know, Jonny, I killed this bear."

"You did?"

"Yep. Me and Captain Coe. He gave me a real gun, and it was bigger than his."

Matt's tale grew taller and taller. Jonny listened with half an ear. He made the chores last as long as he could, getting a certain pleasure out of the feel of the worn pitchfork handle and the smell of dry hay. When his father came in, Matt was sitting on a bale of hay, listening to the real story of the bear hunt.

"It was a foolhardy thing to do, Jonathan," Pa said as he unsaddled the horse. "I should really take a strap to you, but I won't. I'm glad you're home safe. Jed said a man wouldn't have done any better."

Jonny was relieved to get off so easily. He had expected that walloping.

After supper Pa made some reference to little pitchers with big ears, so Ma put Matt to bed. Jonny let him take the new knife sheath to hush his noise.

"Now, Jonny, let's have it," said Pa when Ma came back.

"All of it?"

"Yes, then we'll know what to expect."

Jonny didn't leave anything out, that is, not much. He didn't tell how scared he'd been or how he and Jed had dropped guard and let Jim and Whitey slip up on them. He knew Jed would never tell, and he liked the old man too much to brand him with carelessness.

Jennie's face lit up with pride as she listened. Ma's head was bent over her mending. Pa stood with his back toward his son, looking out into the night. When he finished, Pa turned and his eyes were gray as a storm cloud.

"Jonathan, if Coe ever finds you had anything to do with those horses, your life won't be worth a plugged nickel. You know that? Being a boy won't save you."

"I know."

"He's taken a man's stand, for all he's a boy," said Ma. There was a look of understanding that brought the color into Jonny's blanched face. "It's for the rest of us to stand by him. I'd give my good right arm if he hadn't done it, but he did. It's for us to make the best of it."

Then her tone changed, and she shook her finger under Jonny's nose. "I've got this to say. Martin, neither you or Charles Goodnight won't make me change my mind. Not even if he comes crawling on his knees, begging for provender. Jonny doesn't leave this place till this trouble ends, one way or another."

"Ma, can't I even go to the post?"

"Well, maybe there. But not one step down the Canyon Road. That's final and I want no mouthing out of you. You'll not go down the Canyon Road!"

She slapped her mending into the basket. Jonny opened his mouth to protest but closed it again. This wasn't the time to push matters too far.

"She's right, Jonny," Pa said. "With soldiers nipping at his heels, Coe will be worse than a wounded grizzly."

Jonny went to his room. Matt, with his gun in one hand and the knife sheath in the other, was asleep under the hide. Jonny threw the stinking thing out of the window. He crawled into bed and watched the light from the soldiers' fire dancing on the wall.

The next morning Matt dragged the hide around until Ma couldn't stand it. She told Jonny to take it to town and let Lew show him how to tan it. When he left she had Matt in a tub of soapy water, and he was lifting the sky with his roaring.

Jonny tied his horse to the rack and stuck his head in the door to let Pa know he was there.

Then he ran on down the street to the saddle shop.

The door and windows were open. He could hear loud voices raised in angry protest. Slipping up to the windows, he peered in. The place was crowded. It seemed to him half the men in town were squeezed into the little room.

"This is the way I see it." Lew's voice rose above the others. "We've waited long enough. Where's it got us? Coe moves in closer every time he strikes."

"Organizing a vigilante committee is a serious step." That was Sam Rogers speaking. "It's easy to start a thing like this, but it's mighty hard to disband. Once the men find how easy it can be to settle their private scores under cover of a vigilante committee, nothing can change it."

"It don't always work that way," said Jed. "I've been looking into the matter up in Colorado Territory. Oh, I grant you there's some dirty work goes on, but they do a lot of good, too."

"Have they stopped Coe? That's what they set out to do." Sam's face was as red as a turkey's wattle. "The soldiers are up in arms now. Why not leave it to them?"

"I say we know what has to be done as well as any fetched-in law-man that Hardy's always talking about. Besides, who pays their salaries? We do, that's who. The judge and sheriff—they're only men like us."

"And juries," added the tavern keeper. "We can make a jury right here. We don't have to have a lawyer to make us swear to the truth and nothing but the truth."

"We all know the truth," shouted Jenk.

"Too bad he ain't an Injun. I could use his scalp bounty."

Jonny couldn't see who made that comment, and he didn't recognize the voice.

"Shall we bring it to a vote?" asked Lew.

"What about Hardy?"

"I'll cast Hardy's vote with mine," replied Sam. "I know what he'd say."

"All in favor of forming a vigilante committee, hold up your hand and be counted!"

There was silence as all the heads bobbed about counting the hands.

"Against?"

There was a short pause.

"Sam, looks like you and Hardy stand alone. Now suppose we all meet here tonight and decide what to do."

Jonny tore back to the post and sat down on the steps. His father came to the door.

"You didn't leave your hide with Lew."

"No. There was some men in the shop."

Martin Hardy looked curiously at Jonny.

"So they're planning a committee," he said sadly. Jonny nodded.

"It's been brewing for some time. I did everything I could to stop them. That's why they didn't tell me."

"Sam voted you and him out," said Jonny.

Pa laughed a huge roaring laugh.

"I'm sure glad Sam saw fit to vote for two of us."

Jonny stood up. His head reached a little above his father's shoulder. "I'll vote with you, Pa," he said. "I kind of see things different now, but up there on the Mesa . . . well——"

"If I'd been there, I might've seen it in your light," answered Pa. "Now let's forget about what's going on up at Lew's. Did you forget this is your birthday? Thirteen today. I'm proud you're a Hardy."

Jonny flushed. Praise from his father after all he'd done soothed his spirit. They went into the store and Martin reached into the case and took up a new Winchester.

"I've been thinking it's time you had a man's gun," he said. "Put your old one aside. Matt can have it in three or four years."

Jonny's knees gave way, and he collapsed against the cracker barrel with the gun in his arms.

"Gosh, Pa. Gee, thanks. Oh, gosh a-mighty."

16

Return of the Outlaw

Nerves tightened. As the days passed, Ma lost
the confidence the soldiers' presence had once
brought her. She fretted when one of the children
was out of sight. Jonny was set to hoeing the corn.
A dozen times a day she went out just to catch a
glimpse of him.

He caught her uneasiness. He began to feel eyes
upon him as he worked. He tried to brush the
thought aside as silly and womanish, but it persisted
and grew. Often he stopped work and studied the
sun-baked hills. Nothing moved bigger than a chap-
paral cock, yet he couldn't rid himself of the feeling
of hidden eyes. At times his fear changed to near
panic, and only shame of running stayed his feet.

The soldiers, too, grew surly at their enforced
idleness. They complained and quarreled with each
other. At times they snapped at Matt when his
play disturbed their naps and card games. Matt re-
taliated by throwing rocks whenever he could escape

Ma's eyes. His backside developed a callus from her repeated spankings. But the one-sided battle went on with Matt holding the advantage.

One evening just at dusk a stranger stopped. The soldiers, eager for news, gathered about. The conversation led at once to Coe.

"Haven't heard anything reliable," he told them. "Some folks in Pueblo say he's in jail at Lamar. Others say Denver. One man I talked to said he was still loose, hiding in the Indian caves in the canyon. I wouldn't know. I'm only passing on what I heard."

The soldiers seized this flimsy shred of news as fact. As far as they were concerned, Coe was as good as caught. They had only to find the caves and drag him out. The sergeant caught their optimistic enthusiasm. They called Martin Hardy.

"It don't seem a reasonable hideout," Martin said dubiously. "The country roundabout is dryer than bleached buffalo bones."

Nothing he could say shook their confidence. If Mr. Hardy would guide them, they'd have Coe in chains by tomorrow night.

Pa was still doubtful the next morning, but he promised to act as guide if Jed would keep shop for him. The soldiers could meet him in town later.

"I don't like it," he told the sergeant. "Why don't you leave two or three men here and let the rest go?"

They all rose against this as one man. They'd sat around for ten days waiting for Coe. Now, by the great horned spoon, they wanted to be in on the kill.

"Jonny, take care of the women and Matt," Pa said as he left. "Stay at the house! I'm depending on you."

The soldiers cleaned up camp, caught their horses, and galloped away. When they were out of sight, Jonny went into the house and loaded his gun. Ma didn't ask any questions, which was just as well. This was a man's fight.

He wandered from one window to another. He drew a fresh pail of water and stayed a while to watch Matt digging holes under the plum thicket. He read a month-old newspaper, then whetted his knife on the hearthstones. He was digging in the jar for some leftover corn bread when Jennie called.

"Ma, there's a man coming to the door. He's afoot and looks like a tramp."

Ma opened the door. The man brushed her aside, pushing past her. He closed the door and leaned against it, seeming too tired to stand. He was thin, even gaunt, his yellow hair matted with twigs and dried juniper needles. The stubby growth of beard didn't hide the dirt on his face. Caked mud clung to his scuffed and broken boots.

"Mrs. Hardy, hide me." There was no mistaking the voice. The man was William Coe. "The blasted soldiers are everywhere. My horse fell and broke his leg. I had to shoot him and make my way here on foot. I lost my gun when I swam the river. I've been hiding in the hills behind the ranch for a week, waiting for those lousy yellow-legs to leave. I'm starving. Get me something to eat."

Jonny moved back toward the mantel.

"Jonny!" His mother spoke sharply, and Jonny edged away guiltily. She handed him a fork. "Turn the meat when it's ready; don't let it burn. Jennie, fill the woodbox."

The woodbox was full to overflowing. Bewildered, Jennie looked at Ma, who glanced almost imperceptibly toward the door. Matt was in plain sight, still digging holes. Jennie led him out of sight below the river bank.

Boiling inside, Jonny stood by the stove and jabbed at the meat. Here they were, back to the old way of jigging to Coe's whistle.

Ma mixed biscuits and got out the sand-plum jam. Jonny swore under his breath. Nobody got plum jam unless it was Christmas or a birthday. Ma was dishing up the best, like Coe was King Solomon in all his glory.

Coe rested his head on the table. When the food was placed before him he fell on it like a crippled lobo on a winter-killed deer. Ma urged him to eat, pressing on him more meat, more biscuits, until he pushed back his plate. Bleary-eyed from exhaustion and lack of sleep he stood up.

"Go to the bunkhouse and sleep," Ma said. "The soldiers won't be back till night."

Coe stumbled to the bunkhouse and fell upon

the bed. He was sound asleep instantly. Ma closed the door. She ran to the barn and came back, leading Jonny's pony.

"Get on!" she said.

"Where am I going? Pa told me to stay here and take care of you."

"You're going down the Canyon Road after your father and the soldiers."

"Ma! The Canyon Road!"

Her face was gray as she boosted him into the saddle.

"Suppose he wakes up?" Jonny insisted.

"I've got your gun."

"No, Ma. You can't do that."

Suddenly she pulled him to her and brushed her lips across his cheek.

"Go with God, Jonathan."

When he reached the Canyon Road, Jonny looked back. Ma was sitting on the steps with his gun pointed toward the bunkhouse. He struck the pony, and it leaped forward.

17

The Capture

FOR A TIME Jonny rode blindly, seeing only Ma
crouched with his rifle. Was this the way women
on the wagon trains fought? Without tears, with
only gray faces and cold lips to give away their
fears? Suppose Coe opened the door. Would Ma
shoot? If she didn't, what then?

Coe would show no mercy. He would not con-
sider food and shelter a fit price for her life. He'd
kill her as quickly as he had those people on the
Raton stage. Sooner, for this time he'd kill for his
life and freedom.

Ma was no match for him unless she pulled the
trigger. But would she? The first Bible verse Jonny
remembered learning was "Thou shalt not kill." She
had taught it to him before he could hardly talk.
Could Ma kill? In his heart, Jonny knew she could.
She'd do it for Matt and Pa and all of them. He
must not let this happen.

Jonny struck the pony again, and it flattened to

the road. Wedding Cake Mountain and Camel Rock flashed past. At the Indian camp lank-ribbed dogs gathered yapping for the chase. One gray wolflike beast leaped for the pony's throat. The pony reared and caught the dog a glancing blow with its hoof. The dog rolled, howling and writhing, into the ditch. Jonny didn't look back.

Rounding the point of a hill, he saw two men waiting in the shadow of a boulder. In the instant he flashed past, something about one of them tugged at his memory. A mile or so farther down the road he thought of it. This was the stranger who had brought the rumors of Coe to the soldiers last night. The wolf's running mate had succeeded in sending the hounds on a false scent while the wolf rested.

Matt's words came into his mind. "It's Captain Coe's road." He thought of the young vigilantes who were buried on the Vega. They had been caught trespassing on Coe's road.

Beyond the village of Cimarroncita Jonny began to look for the trail that angled north toward a range of flat sandstone hills. Jed had pointed it out to him on the way back from the Goodnight Camp. It led into a canyon between Twin Buttes. In the walls of this canyon had once lived an ancient race of Indians. Black Wolf said the place was filled with spirits and he and his people avoided it. Some of the whites, too, said the place was haunted. It was outlaw country, and Jonny thought the tales might have been started deliberately to frighten people away.

The pony was beginning to falter and its sides heaved. Jonny pulled it to a walk while he hunted for the trail. He was certain this was the place, but there were so many trails and so many hills. Even grown men lost their way and ended up on the Indian Hunting Ground. Some of them were found later with part of their hair missing.

He rode back and forth, searching for signs that the soldiers had turned off. There had been no rain, and the marks should be as plain as the nose on his face. Then he came upon them and he galloped

off across the prairie. The earth was dotted with prairie-dog holes, and the horse stumbled. Jonny pulled it to a walk again, chafing at the delay, but the risk of a broken leg was too great.

He looked at the sun and wondered how long a man stuffed to his Adam's apple with biscuits and good plum jam would sleep. He tried to reckon how long he'd been gone. From the position of the sun he knew time was running out.

Jonny wandered around jagged boulders and stones of monstrous shapes and sizes and across dry creek beds, gradually working his way toward two tall buttes that rose high above the others. These must be the Twin Buttes of the Indian caves.

When he reached the Mesa walls he was dwarfed by their height. Losing sight of the buttes, he wandered into several canyons, but they all ended in stone walls. The loneliness of the place chilled him. The birds that filled the air each morning and evening with their chattering were silent in the heat of the noon sun.

He came to a wide opening which seemed to lead a long way back. His heart leaped up, for the sandstone walls were pocked with caves. He heard

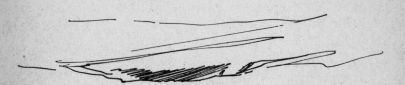

the stamping of fly-pestered horses. His pony whinnied, and the canyon tossed back the echoes. Pa
and the soldiers rode out.

"Jonny!" Pa shouted. "What in thunderation are
you doing here?"

"It's Coe. He's come. He's asleep in the bunkhouse, and Ma's holding a gun on him."

The men didn't wait to hear any more.

"Your horse is tired. Take it slow," Pa cautioned
when they reached the road.

Jonny's answer was a kick in the pony's flanks.
The canyon echoed to the galloping hoofs. With
the sergeant on one side and Pa on the other, Jonny
had no fear of the road that stretched behind them
to Robbers' Roost. As they turned into the ranch
lane he looked for Ma. She hadn't moved. The gun
was still pointed toward the closed door.

As the soldiers surrounded the bunkhouse, Jonny
took the gun from his mother's hands. "I'll take
over now," he said. "This thing gets heavy."

Hearing the commotion Jennie brought Matt out
of hiding.

"What's going on?" he yelled, charging up the
river bank.

"Come out, Coe," the sergeant shouted.

There was no sound from the bunkhouse. The
sergeant shouted again.

"We've got you surrounded! Come out!"

The door opened and Coe, groggy with sleep,
stood blinking in the bright light. One of the soldiers

snapped handcuffs about his wrists. Bewildered, Coe looked around.

"I don't understand. Someone must have told . . ." He saw Jonny's spent pony. "Why, you dirty, little——"

He leaped forward, straining at the handcuffs. Jonny saw him coming but was too dazed to move. Coe struck him across the face with the irons. Bawling like a wounded calf, Matt tore into Coe with teeth and boot heels.

"Don't you hurt my brother," he shrieked.

Coe lifted his hands to strike again. Matt sank his teeth into his thumb. Cursing with pain, Coe tried to shake the boy loose, but Matt clung like a wildcat. His feet left the ground as Coe battered and tossed him about.

Pa leaped forward, grabbed Matt, and gave him a solid smack on the pants. Matt opened his mouth and bellowed. Coe dropped back, nursing his thumb, and Matt whirled on his father.

"I had him licked till you butted in, you big old dodblasted bully," he yelled.

The soldiers roared. Pa laughed too, but he plastered a second smack on Matt's seat. Matt stomped into the house and slammed the door.

Coe cursed and raged like a madman. He swore there was no jail in the country could hold him. He'd escape. When he did, he'd be back. He'd wipe out the whole Hardy tribe from double-crossing Martin to the rat, Jonny, and that little wolf that bit him.

"Your last trip's cut out for you," said the sergeant. "And it won't be back here to the Cimarron country."

He asked Pa to lend him a horse and saddle to take Coe back to Pueblo. The soldiers snapped iron cuffs on the outlaw's ankles and stretched the chain beneath the horse's belly. Promising to return soon, they rode away. Coe still cursed and swore he'd come back.

18

Law Comes to the Canyon

E<small>VEN THOUGH</small> William Coe was gone, there was
still no peace at the Hardy ranch. He had
escaped from forts and jails too many times for
them to believe this was the end. Some day he
would return. A week, a month, a year—Coe would
bide his time.

Pa wore a gun now along with the other men
of the town. When Jonny went back to the corn
hoeing, he carried his rifle. Matt was kept in the
house except when Pa or Jonny could watch over
him.

A month passed and still the soldiers had not
returned the horse and saddle. The townspeople
questioned travelers but always got the old con-
flicting tales. Coe was dead, he was seen in Dodge,
in Denver, he was back at Robbers' Roost.

Then one night the soldiers came. Pa ran out
to welcome them.

"We've been looking for you," he said. "Light

179

and come in. Supper's most ready, and you're welcome to join us."

Jennie hustled about setting more plates on the table while Jonny drew fresh water for them to wash.

"I suppose you heard what happened to our outlaw?" asked the sergeant.

"Not a word," replied Pa. "Did he escape?"

"No, he didn't escape," replied the sergeant, helping himself to the plum jam. "He couldn't escape in chains. Those we put on here were never taken off. He and five of his men, who were captured later in Pueblo, stood trial. They were all found guilty. His men were sent to Denver, and they are now in prison. There was some talk Coe would be sent there too. It stirred up a lot of anger and high feelings, especially among the people who had suffered at his hands. One night the jailer was overpowered by a group of masked men. Coe was taken to a cottonwood tree at the edge of town. His end was the usual one that comes to all men of his kind."

"What about the rest of the Robbers' Roost outlaws?" asked Jonny. "Won't someone try to take Coe's place?"

"I don't think so," answered the sergeant confidently. "There aren't enough left to carry on. We dragged a cannon, a six-pounder, across the plains and hid it at the foot of the Black Mesa. We battered down the hideout. Twenty-five or thirty men ran out when the first shell caved in the roof. Our men were stationed along the Mesa cap rock.

We got most of the outlaws as they ran for the mountain. The few who escaped will be picked up by the law. You can bank on that."

Ma's eyes shone in the lamplight. "The law has come at last," she said softly.

Matt stopped shoveling his food and looked at the sergeant. "What did you say happened to Captain Coe?" he asked.

"He was hanged, sonny. Hanged with his chains on and buried with them."

"That's nice," Matt said, scooping up a spoonful of beans. "He hit Jonny."

About the Story

WILLIAM COE and his outlaw raiders have been dead almost a hundred years. But in the Black Mesa country their mountain retreat still carries the name of Robbers' Roost. Coe and the men who followed him have become legends.

As is the way with legends, truth and fiction have become entangled, and it is hard to separate one from the other. Building a story from such fragile material and a few published records, most of which are contradictory, necessarily leaves much to the imagination.

But the Black Mesa country is real. It lies in the western part of Oklahoma and extends into New Mexico for seventy-five miles. This part of Oklahoma was once known as No-Man's-Land. Soon after the Civil War, William Coe claimed it for his own.

He planned well when he built his stronghold on the banks of Carrizo Creek a short distance from where it merged with the Cimarron River. To the west was New Mexico Territory. Gold had been discovered in the mountains, and settlers were rushing in to homestead the lush farm lands. Along the

Arkansas River to the north lay the main route of the Santa Fe Trail. To the east a branch of this trail angled across No-Man's-Land. This was known as the Cimarron Cutoff, or the Jornada—the Journey.

Along these roads rolled wealth beyond even an outlaw's dreams. Conestoga wagons laden with trade goods destined for Mexico, Santa Fe, and faraway California followed the ridges. They carried also Government rations for the reservation Indians, furs, and gold and silver. Between the wagons plodded the ever increasing number of immigrants. Many had little enough in their creaking wagons. Their scrawny trail-worn cattle were hardly worth the trouble of driving away. But all was grist that came to Coe's mill. Such cattle fattened quickly on his hidden pastures.

Not too far away from the Roost was the Good-night Cattle Trail. In summer thousands of head were pastured on the Capulin Vega—wide, swelling meadowlands which swept from the Black Mesa to the mountains. Texas cattle were easily stampeded and the country was a maze of hidden valleys and canyons where brands could be changed without fear of detection.

Military forts and civil courts of justice were few and scattered, a misfortune which Coe found to his liking. They offered no great threat to him or the men who followed him.

After the war, outcasts from both Northern and Southern armies drifted west. There they banded with men of their own kind, all eager for excitement and quick money. For almost three years under Coe's leadership these outlaws of Robbers' Roost were the scourge of the territories. There was hardly a farmer too poor or a rancher too rich who did not suffer at their hands.

Coe and his raiders were bold. On the other hand, their victims were no weaklings. The weak didn't follow the Santa Fe Trail. The men who homesteaded the Cimarron country were brave and strong and steadfast in their respect for the laws of God and man. And so were the women who stood beside them.

We can assume from the few published records about William Coe that he was a man of ability, one who left little to chance. The close-knit plan which I have attempted to present is purely my own assumption. I have taken the liberty to condense events which must surely have spread over the entire period of Coe's activity into the few weeks encompassed by this story. There is little proof of any of the events other than hearsay and legends. Some of them never actually occurred at all.

The characters, too, are fictional with the exception of the outlaw, William Coe, and Charles Goodnight, who blazed the Goodnight Cattle Trail through New Mexico, Colorado, and beyond.

The plot of the story is based on a well-known tale of the boy, Buddy Emery, whose father owned a ranch and trading post somewhere in the Cimarron

Valley. It was through the efforts of this boy and his mother that William Coe was finally captured.

Too much praise and admiration cannot be given to the wives and the children of those men who tried to build peaceful homes in a lawless land. Behind their almost fanatical dreams of home were faith and courage great enough to forge these dreams into reality.

H.R.

ABOUT THE AUTHOR

HELEN RUSHMORE has lived most of her life in Tulsa, Oklahoma, and can remember it when there were still enough Indians and cowboys in the streets to make life exciting. She and her brothers and sisters, she says, "were more familiar with tales of bank and train robbers, horse thieves and Indian attacks, than we were with fairy tales and nursery rhymes. We younger children played within sight of our home, ready to scamper to safety when Indians rode into town. I think it must have been their long black hair, glittering eyes, and blankets that frightened us."

Traveling in the Black Mesa country in the western part of the state years later, Helen Rushmore heard the legend of the outlaw William Coe and his surprising capture and saw his mountain retreat which is still called Robbers' Roost. She wanted to write a story about the people who left the security of the States to build homes in a new and comparatively lawless land, and she became interested in the young boy and his mother who had brought about the capture of this outlaw.

Miss Rushmore is a teacher-librarian in an elementary school in Tulsa. She has written five popular books for children, including *Chief Takes Over*, which is the most recent.

DATE DUE

GAYLORD			PRINTED IN U.S.A.